COLD CASE

HELP

Cold Case Coalition

CONTENTS

INTRODUCTION, PURPOSE, AND HOW TO USE THIS BOOK

There are as many ways to work cold cases as there are people working them. This book is written for people who are not in law enforcement, such as family members, friends, nonprofits, podcasters, researchers, and former law enforcement.

As one retired detective recently told us, "I've been surprised how hard it is for private citizens to get information on cases." Exactly. You can't pick up the phone and pull a suspect's bank records. You can't get a search warrant. You can't access the National Crime Information Center (NCIC) database. That's why books written for law enforcement have little relevance to what you're trying to do. This book tries to help overcome those hurdles.

We begin with disturbing facts about cold cases in the U.S., such as how much they are underreported and surprising reasons that some cases go cold. Before starting in on specific investigative techniques, we discuss why you'll be doing them – what you'll be looking for in terms of "victimology" and "suspectology," and converting information you find into an all-important timeline.

We then walk you through potential steps in an investigation, beginning with online and other basic searches specific to cold cases.

Because it's so critical, we devote an entire section on how to request case records and what to do if you don't get a full response. We also discuss other information available from courts, prisons, archives, social media, etc.

Organizing and evaluating material is key to understanding your case. We offer ideas, and flag some evidence commonly seen in cold cases that should now be viewed skeptically.

Once you've done initial research on your case, the time will come to talk to witnesses, acquaintances, and perhaps suspects. What do you say? Can you record them? We offer some suggestions.

While most of this book is limited to cold cases, we do discuss actions that should be taken immediately if an adult goes missing and law enforcement has not opened a case. These range from searches to emergency court actions.

No cold case book would be complete without addressing common questions – and misconceptions – about DNA. When does it (not) work? Why isn't it done more?

What if you believe you've solved a cold case but no one will listen? We discuss some options, from simple (seeking higher level review) to extreme (exhumation).

We next discuss the relationship between cold case investigations and innocence challenges. We offer thoughts about getting an innocence program to consider your case, and we explain why prosecutors sometimes resist post-conviction DNA testing.

You should be aware of risks involved with working cold cases. Do you need permission? Can you screw up the case? Can you get sued?

Not all of the research ideas we describe will apply to a single case; in fact, you might end up skipping many of them. We wanted to present a wide range of options.

Because we have a broad range of volunteers, we do some things not discussed in this book. Surveillance. Dredging ponds. Forensic examinations. These options and many others are discussed on our website, ColdCaseHelp.com.

ABOUT US

The Cold Case Coalition is a 501(c)(3) nonprofit run by volunteers. We were founded in 2017 by a lawyer (Karra Porter), private investigator (Jason K. Jensen), and journalist (Tom Harvey). We had been contacted by the family of 6-year-old Rosie Tapia, whose 1995 murder remains unsolved. (That's Rosie on the cover.) We soon heard from others who needed help and our efforts grew quickly. Examples of our activities include:

Cold Case Database. Our first project was legislation creating a statewide database of unsolved homicides and disappearances. "Rosie's Law" requires law enforcement to enter cases that remain unresolved after three years.

DNA. In 2019, we founded Intermountain Forensics, a state-of-the-art DNA lab. Now a separate 501(c)(3) nonprofit, IMF offers advanced DNA testing and no-cost DNA reviews on cold cases. The Coalition also has a Forensic Investigative Genetic Genealogy (FIGG) team that aids qualifying cases from the

IMF Lab in identifying suspects and human remains. In 2022, we were honored to be selected to supervise the historic work of identifying victims of the 1921 Tulsa Race Massacre.

Rewards. We launched a reward program that makes Utah the only state where a reward is offered on every cold case.

Tip Line. Volunteers staff an anonymous 24/7 Tip Line.

Meetings with law enforcement. Survivors often ask us to participate in meetings with law enforcement. We have found that this can enhance understanding by all parties.

Railroads. Our Railroad Murder project is a nationwide database on unresolved railroad-related crimes.

Typical Cold Case Coalition board meeting

Cold Case Talk. We periodically bring light to cases through a podcast, *Cold Case Talk.*

Cold Case Cards. In 2019, we created Utah's first Cold Case Cards, decks of cards describing cold cases that we distribute for free to jails. These cards generate tips when inmates study the cases while passing the time.

Lillie Allen with an image of her daughter's card.
Sheree Allen was murdered in 2005.

Cold Case investigations. Our volunteers have worked on dozens of cold cases, first in Utah and now across the U.S. Our work has led to arrests, identification of bodies and suspects, reopening and closure of cases, reunification of families, packaging of leads for law enforcement, and bringing forgotten cases to light. Some examples are mentioned in this book.

SECTION I
FINDING COLD CASES
TO WORK

The cold case problem is bigger than you think

You may already have a cold case in mind. Perhaps it's a family member or friend. If you don't, many agencies have websites, such as Colorado: https://apps.colorado.gov/apps/coldcase/index.html, Texas: https://www.dps.texas.gov/coldCase/, Bureau of Indian Affairs: https://www.bia.gov/service/mmu/missing-murdered-open-cases, and many others.

Unfortunately, there are thousands of cases to choose from. In fact, the cold case problem is bigger than people realize. The homicide solve rate is declining. One theory is that prosecutors and juries now require higher quality evidence (the "CSI effect"). Another is that "junk" science has been discredited. Another is strained budgets. All are true.

The government estimates there are about 250,000 cold cases in the U.S. That's a low estimate. It omits many cases that are cold cases but aren't included in the statistics.

Cold cases that are not listed as cold cases

Missing adults. Adults generally have a "right to go missing" – to disappear. Without evidence of foul play, it might take years of missed holidays before police will classify the disappearance as suspicious. Members of vulnerable populations might not even be reported missing.

Closed - exhaustion of leads. Detectives run out of leads. The case is then "closed" until new information is received, which might be years (or never).

Closed - death of suspect. Police close the case after a likely suspect is learned to be dead.

On Monday, September 21, 2020, this investigator, along with DETECTIVE LESTER AGUILAR, ID #3568, traveled to Watsonville, California and with the assistance of the Watsonville Police Department arrested RAUL MATA for an arrest warrant charging MR. MATA with one count of First Degree Murder and Burglary with an Assault or Battery. MR. MATA was subsequently booked at the Santa Cruz Correctional Center.

While awaiting extradition to Miami, this investigator learned that MR. MATA stabbed himself in the femoral artery with a pen while in custody. MR. MATA was transported to an area hospital in critical condition.

On Friday, October 16, 2020, this investigator learned that MR. MATA had succumbed to his injuries and was pronounced deceased by medical staff.

Due to death of MR. MATA, this case should be reclassified.

CASE DISPOSITION: EXCEPTIONALLY CLOSED (DEATH OF SUBJECT)

Closed – undetermined. A surprising number of cases have been closed as "undetermined." It might be because the cause of death isn't known, perhaps if only skeletal remains were found. Or it might be unclear whether the manner of death was suicide, accident, or murder. One detective told us that several cases in his department were reclassified as "undetermined" or "unattended death" because the boss was up for a promotion and needed fewer outstanding homicides on the books.

In the following example, a woman was shot in a motel. A frustrated detective spent years fighting his state crime lab and funding woes to remove the dreaded "undetermined" label. He wrote in his report:

There were other issues that brought this case to a halt. The state lab, specifically ███████████ disputed CSI findings as to how this shooting occurred. The state lab had never been to the scene at the time they raised there concerns and had only seen one piece of evidence. I don't have an answer to why or how they came to their conclusion without ever seeing the scene or all the evidence. CSI had a theory based on evidence they collected and observed. With my experience and what I saw I agreed with CSI's opinion as to what happened that day. A meeting was set up at the scene for the Lab and CSI to confer on what the official opinion should be. They were unable to agree on anything.

To add to this ███████████ from the County Attorneys Offices refused to accept any reports on gunshot residue tests that were to be completed by █ ███████████. I did some research and spoke to ███████ at CSI. At the time of this incident ███████ was considered the front runner in knowledge of gun shot residue and in fact invented most of the equipment used by the rest of the country to test it. ███████ told me his decision was based on the fact that ███████ didn't have a college degree.

After almost two years of attempting to find someone to pay for GSR to be

tested the ATF agreed to help. The samples taken by CSI were sent to Foothills Analytical Laboratory. When the results came back they were read by everyone. The results appeared to be promising until Dr. ███ at the M. E. office said he was not happy with the way CSI took the samples. He didn't want to give an opinion because the test was taken in a different way then his office would have collected them. He wouldn't accept the official results in my effort to change his findings to a homicide instead of undetermined.

Closed - arrest. Many agencies close cases when an arrest is made, but don't reopen them if charges are dismissed/never brought, or the suspect is acquitted. Sometimes agencies remain convinced of the suspect's guilt; sometimes it's just an administrative oversight.

Closed – arrest of one defendant. If a crime is committed by 2+ people, a case might be closed when one is arrested. One example is arranged killings, where it is typically easier to identify the person who committed the final act. But until the person who paid for the hit (perhaps with something untraceable at the time like drugs) is identified, the case is technically still cold.

Closed - conviction. A conviction is obviously a good reason to close a case. But cases sometimes stay closed when the conviction is overturned. That might be intentional (law enforcement still think the guy did it, or prosecutors think it's too late to do anything with the case now). Or it might be oversight.

Closed – "exception". Police believe they have their man, but he won't be arrested or charged. Maybe it's because the suspect is already in prison or headed there. In this example, a detective had evidence and an offer to confess by serial killer Robert Silveria (the "Boxcar Killer"), but the prosecutor said no:

```
ON 06/03/96 AT 0830 HOURS, THIS R/O RECEIVED A TELEPHONE CALL FROM "BOB
STOTT" AND WAS INFORMED OF THE CONFESSION OF "ROBERT SILVERIA" CLAIMING THAT
"SILVERIA" COMMITTED THIS PARTICULAR INCIDENT.  DEPUTY "STOTT" REQUESTED A
TRANSCRIPT OF THE TAPED CONFESSION, AND DISTRICT OFFICE WORKSHEET FOR
A"DECLINATION" SINCE  "OREGON" LAW ENFORCEMENT AGENCIES WERE ALREADY
PROSECUTING "SILVERIA" FOR OTHER HOMICIDES, AND SEVERAL OTHER LAW
ENFORCEMENT AGENCIES WERE ALSO IN LINE TO PROSECUTE "SILVERIA" WHO IS
CONSIDERED A "SERIAL" KILLING/MULTIPLY AGENCIES.
   PLEASE SEE DAO #96009791 IN WHICH DEPUTY "BOB STOTT" ISSUED A"DECLINATION"
FOR THE PROSECUTION OF "SILVERIA" FOR THIS PARTICULAR HOMICIDE.   THIS CASE
WILL BE CLOSED BY "EXCEPTION", WITH THE CONFESSION OF PERSON RESPONSIBLE
"ROBERT J. SILVERIA".
```

The detective tried again two years later, but still no luck:

```
ON 01/28/98 AT 1407 HOURS, DETECTIVE QUAKENBUSH CONTACTED THIS R/O AND
STATED THAT INFORMATION BY THE "DEFENSE" FOR "ROBERT SILVERIA" IS NO LONGER
NEEDED. DETECTIVE QUAKENBUSH STATED THAT "SILVERIA" AND HIS ATTORNEY ARE
WILLING TO TRAVEL TO UTAH, AND IN ARRAIGNMENT COURT PLEAD GUILTY TO THIS
PARTICULAR HOMICIDE AS CHARGED BY SALT LAKE CITY D.A. OFFICE.
THIS R/O CONTACTED DEPUTY DISTRICT ATTORNEY "BOB STOTT", WHO REFERRED THIS
R/O TO CHIEF DISTRICT ATTORNEY "BUD ELLETT".
THIS R/O SPOKE WITH CHIEF DISTRICT ATTORNEY "BUD ELLETT" WHO STATED THAT THE
SALT LAKE CITY DISTRICT ATTORNEYS OFFICE IS NOT INTERESTED AT THIS TIME TO
ARRANGE TRANSPORTATION FOR "SILVERIA" IN EXCHANGE FOR A GUILTY PLEAD TO THIS
HOMICIDE.
      THIS CASE WILL REMAIN CLOSED.
```

Closed – refusal to prosecute. Law enforcement think they have enough for charges; prosecutors don't.

UPDATE: October 26, 1994 Detectives followed very strong leads to suspect and have even recovered the weapon used to murder the victim and Thomas Palma. A very strong, probable cause case, was built and presented to the County Attorney. They have refused to issue complaints at this point. The suspect is currently set to stand trial for robbery and rape in Ogden, Utah.

Closed – administrative. We've seen cases closed for informal reasons, such as a suspect leaving the country, adoption of new computer systems (only newer cases were transferred over) and departure of a lead detective.

Closed – no crime. Officials conclude that no crime occurred – perhaps that a death was accidental or self-defense, or a victim committed suicide. These might not be cold cases, but loved ones often seek out second opinions.

Prison deaths. We know of several instances in which prison murders that were not immediately solved were simply closed, the records now destroyed.

Most of these cold cases don't show up on cold case websites, Facebook pages, or podcasts. No one is working them. They're less well known, but as we discuss below, there are advantages to working inactive / closed cases.

When considering a cold case to investigate, it might be useful to consider why the case went cold. If evidence is missing – which happens more often than you might think – law enforcement might not respond even to a promising lead. The case can still be worked, but information might be the only justice the family ultimately receives.

We interact with many members of the public and families. We often hear theories about why cases have gone cold, the most of common of which are:

"The cops don't care because the victim isn't a cute white female." We hear it a lot: "If it was Gabby Petito / Susan Powell / Elizabeth Smart / JonBenét Ramsey, they would have worked harder." Missing White Woman Syndrome is a documented phenomenon in the media. The reasons are unclear. Ratings? Something more disturbing? Disproportionate *media* response to "white woman/girl" cases has been studied (and demonstrated) extensively. But we have not seen similar scholarship studying *police* response to such cases compared to others.

"The cops don't care because Victim has a criminal record / is a sex worker / has a drug history / is a gang member." In the early '90s, it was revealed that the Los Angeles Police Department used the code "NHI" – No Humans Involved – on cases with these types of victims. While we have seen sparse investigations in some of these cases, we've also seen very thorough investigations. It depends on the agency or detective. Some witnesses are also less likely to come forward in these cases because they're at risk (of being arrested, harmed, deported, etc.).

"The cops did it / They are covering it up." We hear this surprisingly often. Law enforcement/ex-law enforcement are indeed suspects in some cases. As one high profile example, the Golden State Killer was ex-police. But it's not a common reason why cases go cold.

"The cops have too many cases." True.

So, why do *we* think most cases go cold?

Workload / Money. New cases come in and budgets are limited. It's pure economics. Suppose it's important to interview someone in person across the country. $800 for airfare and hotel aren't in the budget. The case stalls. DNA testing is even steeper. (We explain why in our Myths and Realities of Cold Case DNA section.)

Delayed reporting / opening of a case. Delays in reporting or opening a case can be fatal to the investigation. For example, *see* our Missing Persons section below (explaining how cell phone location data is destroyed after 90 days). By the time it's clear that foul play is involved, the trail is cold.

Delayed identification. In many instances, a delay occurred between finding and identifying a body. Because the victim's identity is a critical starting point, this impacts the investigation. In this example, more than a year passed before a 1982 murder victim was identified:

```
WOULD HAVE BEEN CARRYING A "JANSPORT" SELF CONTAINED BACK PACK
AND PACK FRAME GREEN IN COLOR, LIGHT BLUE DOWN SLEEPING BAG,
EARPHONE AM-FM RADIO, LIGHT BLUE DOWN JACKET...STUFFED INTO ONE
SLEEVE.  MIGHT HAVE BEEN CARRYING A WELL WORN BLACK LEATHER
JACKET. WOULD HAVE HAD A SMALL ADDRESS BOOK....COVER POSSIBLY
MISSING, AND COULD HAVE HAD SOME OTHER COLD AND WARM WEATHER
CLOTHING...  I ADVISED MRS.        THAT NONE OF THE ITEMS SHE
DESCRIBED HAD BEEN FOUND WITH THE BODY, TOLD HER ALSO THAT THE
INVESTIGATION HAD BEEN STYMIED BY THE FACT THAT IT TOOK US SO
LONG TO MAKE A POSITIVE ID OF THE VICTIM.
```

Mistakes. Prosecutors might be concerned that evidence will be thrown out because of an improper search or interrogation, or questionable securing of a crime scene.

Statute of limitations. Murder has no statute of limitations. However, related lower-level crimes do, such as manslaughter, negligent homicide, desecration of a body, and obstruction of justice. A prosecutor might be concerned that the evidence doesn't rise to the level of proving murder.

Uncooperative, unlocatable, or unidentifiable witnesses. Witnesses might have been worried about retaliation, married to the suspect, concerned about being arrested or deported, or just hard to locate.

INFORMATION BULLETIN

TO:	Burlington Northern Santa Fe	NUMBER: 030-95
	Resource Protection Team	
		DATE: 11/03/95

Name:	*Numerous subjects* (see additional pages)
	Subject #1 - True name unknown. Alias: Dogman Tony, Hugh W. Ross, Hugh T Ross, Hugh P. Ross, John Lee, Steven J. Hanson, Dennis A. Boxter, Guy Alfred Matthews, Joseph C. Cambell, Steven Joseph Cambell, Steven John Hanson, David Hunn, Dennis Baxter, Christopher Matthews, John G. Boris, John Stanley Boris, Christopher Dune Roberts, Christopher Jay Roberts, Anthony Vincent Vaughn.
DOB:	11/05/50, 12/07/52, 01/15/50, 05/31/51, 08/25/47 (35-45 yrs old)
Race/Sex:	White/Male
Hair/Eye Color:	Unknown
Hat/Wgt:	5'10"/200 lbs.

Apart from notoriously uncooperative witnesses - who could "catch out" and be across state lines within hours - railroad murders often involve train riders using numerous fake IDs.

Known suspect but insufficient evidence. While law enforcement (and the public) might be frustrated at times, prosecutors have a duty to ensure that cases are strong. As former homicide prosecutor Creighton C. Horton II wrote in *A Reluctant Prosecutor*, "One of the most difficult things you must do as a prosecutor is be willing to decline a case if it's not there, despite the considerable pressure that can be brought to bear to induce you to file." He cites an example of a county attorney who was roundly criticized for not charging a murder suspect. Years later, the true killer was revealed by DNA.

Tunnel vision. Law enforcement or family might zero in on one individual or theory, diverting attention from other possibilities. It might be because they relied on a witness's statement that turned out to be wrong, a polygraph, criminal history, or other factors that didn't provide the answer.

Scientific and technological limitations. Many cases are cold for the simple reason that DNA wasn't a known tool. It was first used to solve a U.S. murder in 1987. Many crime labs did not have DNA capability until the mid- to late 1990s. Samples needed to be much larger and less degraded than today. DNA can be extracted from clothing, jewelry, shell casings, and even (according to a May 2023 report) thin air.

Fingerprinting was less precise than it is now (Google carbon dot powders and biosensors), and there wasn't a national database until the 1990s. The national data bank for bullet data (National Integrated Ballistic Information Network (NIBIN)) wasn't created until the early 2000s. Financial records took days to access, instead of minutes. Surveillance video was nonexistent or grainy. Phones were not portable and couldn't track our movements. There was no internet.

SECTION II

VICTIMOLOGY, SUSPECTOLOGY, AND TIMELINES

VICTIMOLOGY AND SUSPECTOLOGY

As you research your case and interview people, one goal is to better understand your victim, missing person, or potential person(s) of interest. Remember that, theoretically at least, anyone can be a suspect until ruled out – even if that person asked you to research the case. More on that later.

When you're doing the research that we describe below, look for information that will help you understand "victimology" and its counterpart, "suspectology". When you're reading a news article or court record, what does it tell you about the victim's history, personality, habits, acquaintances, employment, interests, and so forth?

Was your missing person trusting so she might accept a ride from a stranger? Did she work in an area where a similar crime occurred a week earlier? Did she go to bars, hike, bowl, go garage saling? Was your suspect a truck driver so you should extend your search to other states? Did he have a history of violent crimes? Was he left handed? Did he move suddenly after the incident? Was he asked about this case in an unrelated parole hearing? You'll pay attention to this kind of information when you are using the research methods described in later sections.

When studying subjects (victims or suspects), consider:

- *Relationships.* Did the subject have relationships? When? Who? Remember that stranger-on-stranger crimes are relatively rare. Had the victim broken up with anyone at any time? Are there ex-significant others who might want to talk now? In one case, we discovered that a subject was secretly married to two women when one was murdered. Relatives of a third ex-wife provided valuable information including a pseudonym he used on social media.

- *Relatives.* Family members might know a victim's habits, interests, etc. They might have a hairbrush, envelope, or other object with the relative's DNA. Tracing all descendants is also important because one child might have been adopted or have misattributed paternity (a Non-Paternity Event), which can skew the results of DNA testing.

- *Other family history.* Family histories and names can be clues. In one case, we were confirming that our person of interest changed his name around the time of a 1980s murder. Tracing his family tree, we discovered that his unusual new name was a combination of an uncle-in-law and a grandfather.

- *Employment.* What did the victim do for a living? Did he change jobs recently / frequently? Did the employer provide death benefits that might be a motive? Coworkers know things, and they tend to remember when a colleague is murdered or disappears. In one of our cases, an 86-year-old former office manager provided key information about a victim's work schedule and statements made shortly before her death 30 years earlier.

- *Social life.* Did the victim use dating services? Go to clubs, gyms, or hobby groups? Who were her friends? How did the victim usually communicate? Depending on the age of the case, it might be phone calls, letters, email, Instagram, gaming apps, etc.

- *Residences.* Residences might link someone to a crime scene. They might reveal neighbors with information. In one case, tracking all of a suspect's prior residences revealed that he once lived in the same household as a close friend of our victim.

- *Home life.* Where did the victim live? And where before that (and before that)? Was he behind in his rent or mortgage payments? Did neighbors notice any visitors or routines? Did he have parties, or was he quiet? Were any lawn care, maintenance, or other services performed recently?

- *Personality/Interests/Activities.* Was the victim an extrovert? What did she like to do in her spare time? Did she work out? Walk her dog? Go to the beach? Engage with social media? Eat out? Order in? Did they have a car, ride the bus, or use ride share apps?

- *Risk factors.* Did your victim hang with risky people? Did he do drugs? Did he engage in criminal activity? Was your victim a sex worker? Would she fall for a "lost puppy" scheme? Was there anything that might make them a target? Had the victim experienced any other crime, such as a burglary or vandalism? Had any unusual or stressful events recently occurred?

- *Education.* Schoolmates often know things about the victim's family dynamic, friends, extracurricular activities, etc. (and often were never interviewed).

- *Court history.* Did your subject have a criminal history? Had he been arrested, incarcerated, or sued?

The same types of information can be helpful in evaluating suspects. Given that most killers are previously known – at least briefly – to their victims, building bios on potential suspects is critical. (Google the "circle theory" of forensics.) This is especially true when looking for a body. In a majority of cases, bodies are disposed of somewhere familiar to or near the suspect such as highways (for truck drivers), dumpsters, or wooded areas. Track the suspect's post-event actions – did he suddenly change his routine? Was he later convicted of a serious crime?

TIMELINES

While researching your case, you will be compiling or planning a timeline. Timelines are critical to investigations. We have also found timelines to be an effective way to submit leads to law enforcement.

No particular format is required. You can create separate timelines for victims and persons of interest or do a single one. Regardless of the format, all of our timelines contain these elements:

- *Sources.* Identifying all sources of information helps with documentation and evaluation of discrepancies.

- *Dates/times.* When identifying a date or time, we indicate whether it is guesstimated or more reliable. If the witness or document states an exact time, we explain the reasoning. For example, we might write "11:00 (witness remembers telling suspect he did not want to go to lunch because it was only 11 o'clock)".

- *Birth/marriage/relationships/births of children.*

- *Criminal arrests / trials / incarcerations.* A woman told us that her ex-husband murdered an unhoused person. Our timeline quickly confirmed that her ex was not paroled until a week after the murder.

- *Leading up to the crime.* What happened in the weeks before the crime? Did the victim go out of town? Start a new job? File for divorce? Be specific.

- *Day(s) of incident/disappearance.* This section is *very* detailed. One example: Police told us they ruled out a suspect because he did not have time to get to the location. From our minute-by-minute timeline, we discovered that one witness had called back the next day to say she had misspoken about the time. The corrected information did not make it to the assigned detective. It opened up a 2-hour window for the suspect to drive there and back – plenty of time.

- *Notes / comments.* Notes and comments can include questions, inconsistencies, and suggestions for follow up. Err on the side of over-inclusiveness – remember that even seemingly inconsequential details might later become important.

No specific format is required. It can be a Word doc, Google doc, or anything else that works for you. Spreadsheets are excellent for timelines. Timelines should be electronic and searchable, not handwritten.

In this simple example, the volunteer created a table in Word, and included sources (identified by initials) within her chronology. In her notes column, she included comments, questions, and areas for follow up.

9/8/1986: DAY OF DIANA'S MURDER	
6:10 – Gilbert borrows niece's gray car. Ilene says it had a little more than ¾ tank that morning; later describes tank as "practically full" when left with Gilbert (*IG*).	Police reports do not state the make/model, just that it was a "fast back" type without a trunk but instead a "rear lift window"; gray seat covers and maroon floor mats.
6:50 – Gilbert drops niece off at IRS building. Niece says she usually dropped Gilbert off, but this morning he said he needed the car. This was something he had done only twice before (*IG*).	IRS building was near DDO, both in area of 12th South. Police did not ask Gilbert why he wanted the car that day. At some point that a.m., Gilbert called an on-base "cab" to take him from one building to another – why, if he had a car?

Another volunteer prefers Excel spreadsheets for his timelines. Columns typically include date and time, event/activity, notes, sources, and comments.

One Coalition member works primarily with Airtable (http://www.airtable.com) and Google MyMaps. (Her work is so impressive that detectives asked her to show them how to do it in other cases.) Columns can be created in a way to automatically accumulate information in separate tabs as it is entered. For example, when she put fictitious Lisa's name in the Persons / Places / Things column, an entry for Lisa was automatically created for the People/Place/Thing tab. If she types Lisa's name in the P/P/T column in another event row (such as row 4), Lisa's name will pop up, and she can select it. When she looks at Lisa's P/P/T tab, it will now have all of the events that she selected. Here's a sample (segmented due to size):

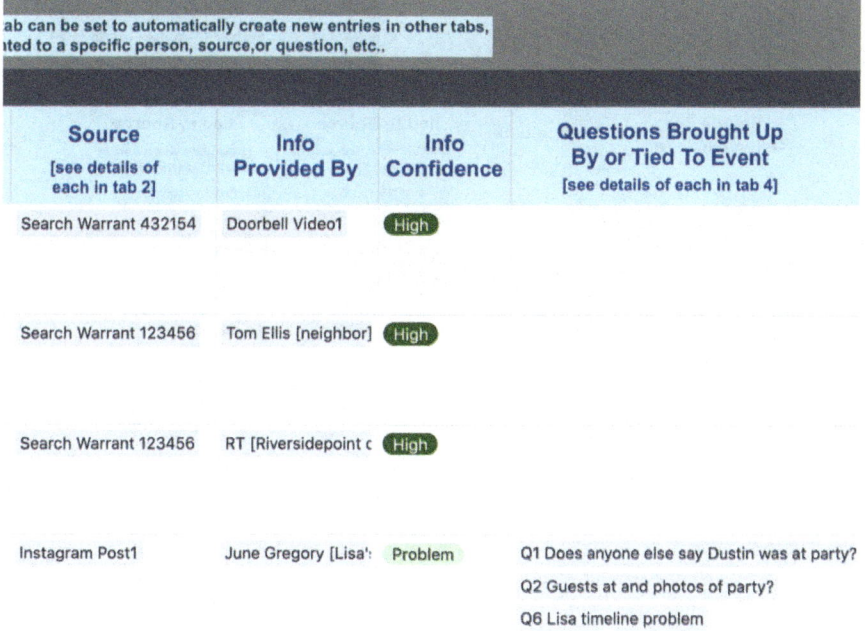

	Day and time of Event	Time Variance/ Confidence	Event	Persons, Places, Things Involved [see details for each in tab 3]
1	July 4, 2015	09:30 Exact	Robert Jones and girlfriend Shauna Miner argue with Robert's ex, Lisa Smith, on front porch of Robert's home (3147 S. Lee St, Clinton)	Robert Jones [victim] Lisa Smith [ex gf] Shauna Miner [gf]
2	July 4, 2015	10:30 About	Robert and Shauna leave for Riverpoint Park camping trip around 10:30am. Per Google maps drive time usually 1hr 45 min. (Riverpoint Park is 85 miles NE of home in Clinton)	Robert Jones [victim] Shauna Miner [gf]
3	July 4, 2015	12:42 Exact	Robert and Shauna check in at Riverpoint Park camp host desk. Assigned camp site 19-A. Robert's truck and small travel trailer. Camp host doesn't see anyone else with them.	Robert Jones [victim] Shauna Miner [gf] RT [Riversidepoint camp host]
4	July 4, 2015	14:00 ?	Lisa Smith arrives at a family party in Perryville per Lisa's mother. (Pville is 115 miles SE of Clinton with usual drive time of 2hrs 5 min. Pville 141 miles south of Riverpoint Park. Drive through Red Fork alright for either)	Lisa Smith [ex gf]

Source [see details of each in tab 2]	Info Provided By	Info Confidence	Questions Brought Up By or Tied To Event [see details of each in tab 4]
Search Warrant 432154	Doorbell Video1	High	
Search Warrant 123456	Tom Ellis [neighbor]	High	
Search Warrant 123456	RT [Riversidepoint c	High	
Instagram Post1	June Gregory [Lisa':	Problem	Q1 Does anyone else say Dustin was at party? Q2 Guests at and photos of party? Q6 Lisa timeline problem

The Sources column and tab work the same way. She can also add extra columns for a source file/screenshot, links to online sources, notes, etc.

Cold Case Help

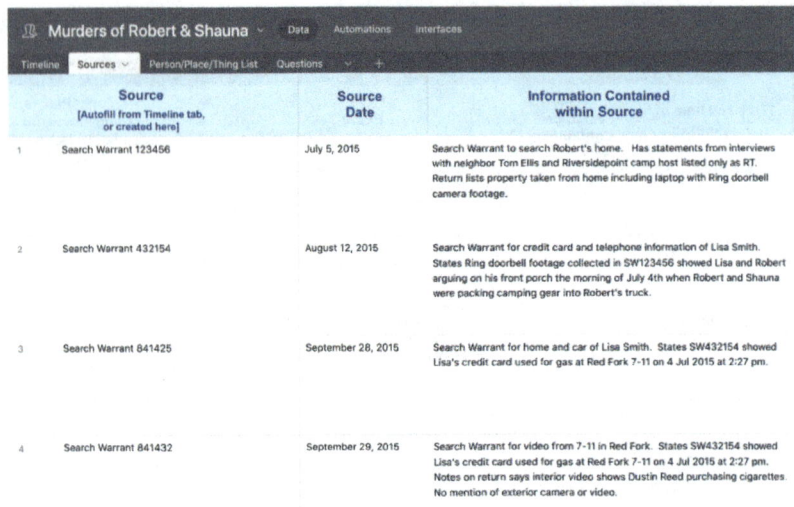

An additional advantage is that Airtable is collaborative; multiple people can contribute at the same time. (Examples of this Board member's amazing timelines can be found on our website, ColdCaseHelp.com.)

Now it's time to dig in.

SECTION III
HOW TO GET STARTED

You have a case you want to work on. How do you start? First, while this might be hard if you've waited decades for answers, we recommend avoiding publicly criticizing prior efforts. It seldom moves the case forward, and it might make it harder to get information. Also, there might be things you don't know about the original investigation. There are more productive ways to generate renewed interest in the case, as discussed later.

If you knew the victim or family, you might start with more information than others. But your investigation should still be open-minded and demonstrate objectivity and thoroughness.

Cold Case Help is divided into sections illustrating one possible order of activities. It assumes you have the patience to research your case thoroughly before taking the next steps. Some folks, such as private investigators, might just go with their gut (or limited client budgets) and jump right into interviews. That's certainly not unreasonable. As a group, though, we feel that one advantage of a case being "cold" is that you have time for a deeper dive, better preparing you for later steps. That's how we approach most cases. It takes longer, but it permits a deeper analysis when we present our leads to law enforcement.

We'll get started now with basic online research you'll want to do when you start working on any cold case.

GENERAL ONLINE COLD CASE RESEARCH

As with many things, a key tool in gathering information about cold cases is Google.[1] Entire books are written about using Google, and there are helpful articles like https://www.lifehack.org/articles/technology/20-tips-use-google-search-efficiently.html. We can't go into that kind of depth here, but here are some Google tools ("operators") we use frequently when researching cold cases:

Phrase/name. Quote marks limit a search to a specific phrase or name. NOTE: Arrestees were sometimes identified by their full names even if that is not how they were known to the public before then. (Think John Wayne Gacy.) It helped distinguish them from others with the same first and last names, but it means you must include searches with and without a middle name and sometimes initials.

All words / excluded words. Adding a + to your search returns produces results with each term. ("Marilyn Harris" +Dallas). A minus sign produces results without that word ("Marilyn Harris" -Iowa).

Date-related. Date restrictions might be helpful. One type is limiting search results to information posted online during certain time ranges. After typing your search on the main Google.com page, clicking the "Tools" button in the upper right corner generates a drop-down menu that says "Any Time." Click on the drop-down arrow and change it to "last year," "last month," or custom date range (for example, 2009-2011). You can also search for text containing a specific date

---

[1] Other search engines include Bing and DuckDuckGo, but Google is the most popular.

range. For example, "Rosie Tapia" +2003..2005 would produce results where the text specifically includes 2003, 2004, or 2005.

Related words. Adding a ~ produces similar or related words. For example, "Diana Frederick" +~arrest will produce results with words like charged, criminal, etc.

Wildcards. Adding an asterisk * produces results within a certain number of words. Murray * Miller produces results where Murray is within one word of Miller. Adding an * within a word produces alternate spellings.

Image / Video searches. You can limit searches to images and video by simply clicking those options on your Google search. You can also do a reverse-image search by right-clicking on a photo and selecting "Search Image with Google." We haven't found reverse image searches too helpful except when images are identical, which can help find websites that talk about your case/victim/suspect (or identify copyright infringement if an image is being used without permission.)

News search. When looking for general news articles on the internet, searching at news.Google.com might be more useful than a general Google search. As with a regular Google search, you can limit the date range.

There are many more Google tricks; you should familiarize yourself with them before doing more in-depth cold case research. If you're computer confident, you might consider some of the OSINT (open-source intelligence) hacks in books like *OSINT Techniques: Resources for Uncovering Online Information* by Michael Bazzell.

NOTE: We have not yet found artificial intelligence programs like ChatGPT (http://www.chatGPT.com) to be helpful in cold cases. They do summarize online (mis)information, but a cold case investigator must independently evaluate information and records that are not usually available on the internet. It can be useful to ask ChatGPT for the sources that were used in its summary. That might alert you to online sources that you can check directly. ChatGPT is also helpful in drafting documents like authorizations and record requests, as discussed below.

"People finder" sites

For more in-depth background, we start with one or more of these sites:

- Truthfinder.com, BeenVerified.com, Spokeo.com, WhitePages.com (Premium), and other online "people" searches. Most of these require payment, but FamilyTreeNow.com is growing and free.

- TLO (http://www.TLOxp.TLO.com). This search engine is populated by the credit bureau TransUnion. It is a deep search and requires a subscription by eligible subscribers (law enforcement, private investigators, attorneys).

- http://www.LexisNexis.com (Public Records). This is another deep search program. Users aren't as restricted as TLO, but it requires a subscription. Many court libraries and law firms have LexisNexis subscriptions, but a people search is usually a separate cost.

NOTE: If you have access to multiple sites, search them all, and remember to search variations. When identifying one victim, the official spelling did not yield any current records. Searching with a slightly different surname was the key. TruthFinder revealed a speeding ticket in the county of interest in the same year. BeenVerified did not have the ticket, but showed VINs for the vehicle that were useful when the car was later sold in a different state.

Crime websites

Check to see if any online groups have posted about or are working on your case. Some top sites include:

Reddit.com. This is a good resource. On the main www.Reddit.com page, just type a search into the box at the top. You can search by interest, person, etc. "Rachelle Arenaz" pulls up a summary we posted about this 1979 murder. Discussions are often thoughtful. When posting, you can cite private knowledge, but you should at least generally describe your source(s), and you must link to at least one online source that cannot be social media. It could be a government cold case site.

Websleuths.com. This site's members make efforts to report developments on cold cases. Posting rules are restrictive, so discussion tends to center around public sources such as media reports.

Private pages. Many families and organizations create websites or social media pages on cases. An excellent example is Justice for Brian Dean Housley, https://www.facebook.com/groups/383363132388775/, maintained by Brian's mother. Some pages cover all cold cases in a particular area. The Facebook page Oklahoma Cold Cases, for example, has 69,000 followers. Check these types of pages – and study the comments. They often contain theories or names of potential contacts.

Documentaries and podcasts

It's worth searching for podcasts, documentaries, and TV shows about your case. You can add +podcast or +documentary, etc., to your Google search. Or search http://www.ListenNotes.com or any podcast app.

We recommend looking for any local case during the same era because it might shed light on the case you are working. As an example, a podcast about the 1978 murder of Anthony Adams in Salt Lake City is likely to mention that evidence in several cases from that time has been lost.

Books about your case

If you're working on a case that hasn't had a lot of attention, you're unlikely to find a book about it. It's still worth checking http://www.WorldCat.org, Amazon.com, or Google just in case. (Remember to search the "author" category. Interviewees

Caution!

Take what you hear / read on the internet with a grain of salt. How thorough does the research seem to be? Is it a summary of media, or does the poster/ broadcaster appear to have records or other sources? Is she objective, or does she seem to accept as true everything the family or a detective or a witness says?

are sometimes listed as authors of the recording.) We discuss later why you should also look for other books not related to your case.

Newspaper and Other Media Research

Many of you are familiar with newspaper searches, but there are some tricks specific to cold cases. We'll start with suggestions for finding online newspapers and newspaper articles to search. NOTE: "Libraries" include public, university, college, and Family History Center libraries.

Search engines and newspaper sites. Many news articles, even decades old, can be accessed through simple Google searches. For example, decades of articles from Salt Lake City's *Deseret News* are available for free online.

Some local newspapers offer an archive service on their websites. You should check all newspapers in the area. Lists of newspapers can be found on Wikipedia. For example, https://en.wikipedia.org/wiki/List_of_newspapers_in_Oregon, produces a list of current and defunct Oregon newspapers. Another source is *Chronicling America*'s finder aid, https://chroniclingamerica.loc.gov/search/titles/, which has a complete and current list of newspapers that can be searched by city/county/state. (The site itself only has limited newspapers, mostly predating 1923.)

Local sites. If you're lucky, a state or local organization has a site like California Digital Newspapers https://cdnc.ucr.edu/ or Utah Digital Newspapers https://digitalnewspapers.org/. These sites offer – for free – a wide range of statewide papers and date ranges.

Newspapers.com Publisher Extra. A scaled down version of Newspapers.com is included with Ancestry.com. For cold cases, however, subscribing to Newspapers.com's Publisher Extra version is essential. It may be available for free in some libraries. The Publisher Extra version has a much wider range of newspapers and dates. NOTE: Don't use Newspapers.com's "clip" feature unless you've changed your settings to "Private." Otherwise, anyone can track what you're searching.

NewspaperArchive.com. This is a large collection that overlaps with Newspapers.com but is worth checking. It's expensive, but available for free at many libraries.

GenealogyBank.com. This pay site focuses more on historical papers, but it has some modern coverage. It also has a large obituary collection (also partially available on FamilySearch.org). It is available for free in some libraries.

Newsbank. Older newspapers in some areas (for example, Houston) are available only through www.Newsbank.com, which does not offer individual subscriptions but is free in many libraries.

If you can't find historical versions of a paper online, call or email the newspaper. They usually know how you can access old copies. And don't forget that many newspapers are available on microfilm at local libraries even if they aren't online yet.

Tricks for searching newspapers in cold cases

Names. You can begin with the victim's name, but that's never enough. Perhaps the victim is not yet identified, or the family hasn't been notified.

Misspellings. Assume the victim's name is misspelled, even if it's a common name. Sometimes the newspaper gets the name wrong, perhaps because someone misheard it wrong or was reading difficult handwriting.

Joe O. Krlotnik, Skidmare 23
Ana Ravnikor, Skidmore 16

Someone couldn't read the chicken scratch: this Kansas groom
was actually Joe Oplotnik (no middle initial)

Also, keep in mind that these newspapers have been scanned (OCRed), which is imperfect technology. An N might be read as a U. The name might be hyphenated or split into two lines. Get creative. Searching for "Thaxton," we've found results under Thackston, Thax ton, Thaxten, Thaxtou, Thackstov, Thavton, fhackston, lhaxton, etc.

Other names. Search for other names or words potentially associated with the case. For example, search the lead detective's name if you know it. He might comment about "last week's homicide" or "the recent sniper attack," which you know is your case.

Addresses. Addresses are frequently included in stories about crimes. Consider how it might be shorthanded or referred to locally. (A crime that occurred at 324 East 4289 South might be referred to as the "300 block," "42nd South," etc.) Neighbors can be found in city directories, so their names and addresses can be searched too.

Town or area (if small or unusual). Searching for "St. Louis" might not be helpful, but "Snoqualmie" or "Juab" might. In rural areas, the location of a body or crime is commonly described in reference to a nearby town or landmark ("2 miles from Mills Junction").

Description of crime or suspect. We usually search for generic descriptors common in crime articles. Examples include: homicide, "found dead", "slay suspect", murder, victim, suspect, vanished, stabbed/stabbing, foul play, body, disappeared/disappearance, "missing woman" (man, child, teen), "attempt to locate", "human remains", skeletal, mutilated, "police department" (spokesman, detective), unsolved, "no suspects," etc. NOTE: some disturbing crime signatures, such as genital mutilation, are not explicitly described. Look for euphemisms.

Date ranges. Searches for the victim's name should not have an end date. Articles continue to be written long after the crime:

Year-end summaries. Newspapers used to prepare annual summaries of the prior year's homicides. Reporters would call law enforcement for updates that weren't reported elsewhere.

Anniversaries / retrospectives. Some stories are updated for anniversaries, birthdays, or stories about unsolved cases in general. Articles about a detective's retirement might ask about cases that still bother her.

Arrests / trials / appeals. Stories are often updated when something new happens in the process, such as an arrest, court appearance, trial, or appeal. Notices used to be printed in local newspapers for upcoming parole hearings, usually mentioning at least the name of the prisoner, prison number, and sometimes the crime for which they were convicted.

TV and radio archives

Local TV stations have archives of their news programming, but it varies wildly. Until the late '70s, many stations did not record most of their broadcasts, so there is no record of what was aired. Also, TV stations change ownership over the years, and might not purchase or keep their predecessor's archive. Locating TV news archives can be as simple as calling the station.

NOTE: Be careful before asking a station for footage. They might contact the original law enforcement agency. The agency might do a quick "review," recharacterize the case as "active," and deny you any records. In most cases, you should submit a records request *before* creating renewed interest in a dormant case. (See the next section.)

Some TV stations donate content. As one example, 1981-1998 daily news broadcasts by KSTW in Tacoma, Washington, and 1960s-2013 raw footage and interviews from Seattle station KIRO are housed in the University of Washington's Special Collections.

Radio content is harder to find. Daily content was rarely recorded or retained. In one triple murder case we've worked for years, a key issue is when news of the murder first came over the radio. We've had no luck verifying that.

Books about other cases

Books about crimes in the same area often give insight. They might describe limitations or controversies within law enforcement at the time. Did a series of bombings draw investigators off other cases? Were there internal disputes among detectives? Did the medical examiner turn out not to have a medical degree (true story)?

Books about other crimes paint a picture of how things were. It's hard for some to imagine a world without cell phones, without 911, without personal computers, when police reports were handwritten. *Death Roads: The Story of the Donut Shop Murders* (Orvel Trainer, 1979) illustrates how a family of traveling criminals could support themselves and evade capture – while committing at least 22 horrific murders – in the early 1970s.

While researching a puzzling prison death, we almost skipped *Doing Time at the Utah State Prison in Draper, Gunnison, and AP&P* (Laddie Pruett, 2014) because the author wasn't hired at the prison until after the death we were investigating. We're glad we did check, because the author describes what he was told about it by fellow guards.

If you're researching the Atlanta Child Murders, *The List* (Chet Dettlinger and Jeff Prugh, 1983) is a must read. Whether you agree with the authors' conclusions or not, the degree of detail about the murders is remarkable.

In Plain Sight: The Startling Truth Behind the Elizabeth Smart Investigation (Tom Smart and Lee Benson, 2006), sheds light on how some departments approached missing person investigations and families in the early 2000s.

These are just a few examples of books we've found useful. Get creative. You never know what you might find.

SECTION IV

GETTING RECORDS

You need records. Media accounts are not enough. They're often wrong and always incomplete. In this section, we'll describe how to request records from the government (most often a police department, sheriff's office, or other law enforcement agency).

After you submit your request, you might get a call from a detective and learn some insight. (Or get yelled at – we've had both.) If you get the good kind of call, show gratitude and repay the favor by honoring confidentiality requests.

Unfortunately, a more common response is this: The records clerk calls down and says a request has come in. The homicide detective says, "It's an open case. They can't have anything." Your request is denied.

Is that how it's supposed to work? Not necessarily. In many states, you're entitled to *some* records even on "open" cases. It varies from state to state. Here are some examples.

Washington's Public Records Act has been read to allow withholding of documents in "pending" cases until the case has been presented to a prosecutor (even if the prosecutor declines charges and sends it back for more investigation). After that, the police must show how disclosure of each document would interfere with its investigation.

In a 2015 case, the New York City Police Department sought a blanket exemption for a 27-year-old cold case under New York's Freedom of Information Law. The court said no, writing, "NYPD has not cited to a single fact which would make this case any different from any other unsolved 'cold case' homicide. NYPD tries to raise a barrier that would bar all open criminal case files, without exception, from FOIL review. As previously noted, this cannot be the intent of the Legislature in enacting FOIL."

The Georgia Supreme Court has interpreted that state's law to allow police to withhold documents from any "pending investigation." If the case has been closed, however – even if it is unsolved – documents must be disclosed. (You can see why it is important to submit your records request before doing anything that might reopen an investigation.) Initial Incident Reports must also be disclosed in all cases.

In one 50-year-old cold case, an Illinois court rejected a police department's attempt to withhold everything, writing: "Understandably, [the agency] would prefer to claim exemptions over their entire files rather than sift through thousands of documents to redact exempt matters and disclose whatever is left. Unfortunately for [the agency], the law itself does not authorize such a generic approach."

In Utah, you're entitled to "Initial Contact Reports," which is much broader than the name suggests. *Any* report that contains the following type of information is considered an Initial Contact Report: Nature of complaint, incident, or offense; Date, time, and location; actions taken in response to the incident; general nature of injuries or damages; identity and contact information for persons charged or arrested; and identity of responding public safety personnel.

In other words, whether you can get records and what you can get depend on your state. If you're having trouble navigating your state's laws, feel free to contact us; we compile cold case record laws and court cases.

We've seen law enforcement refuse any disclosure – even to family – on a case more than 50 years old. Meanwhile, witnesses, suspects, and loved ones are passing away with no answers. If this is a problem in your state, consider asking your legislature to enact a time limit for keeping cases private, at least from family or licensed professionals. Even if the bill doesn't pass, the public debate might be informative.[2]

How to get police reports and other government records

The first thing you need to do is figure out each agency that might have records about your case. There might be more than one. A common example is when a homicide victim is initially reported as a missing person. There usually are at least two case files: the original missing person report where the person was reported missing or last seen, and the homicide report where the body was found. NOTE: Missing persons cases are typically reclassified as "closed" when the person or their remains are found.

Agencies sometimes help each other on investigations and might have separate files. That is especially common with

---

[2] We feel that exceptions could extend to licensed professionals because they are subject to regulation (and discipline) if they do something improper, such as disclosing restricted documents.

city/town police departments and county sheriff's offices. Look for references to other agencies mentioned in reports or news stories.

As you've seen, public records are governed by your state law. If state statutes say a record must be produced, local agencies cannot withhold it. NOTE: You are entitled to ask for records regardless of whether you live in the state.

It would be nice if every public record site was as easy to figure out as Albuquerque's (Google Albuquerque +"public records"):

or Denver's (Google Denver +"police records"):

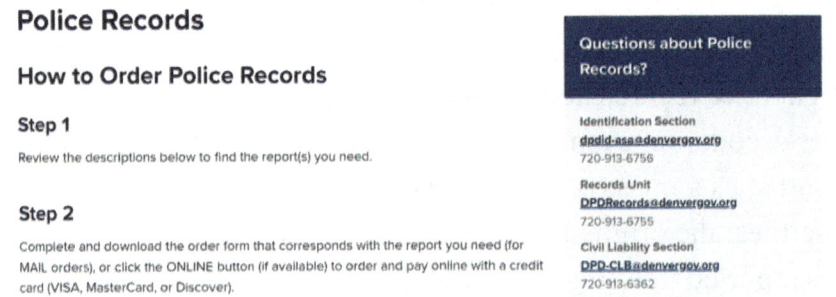

Unfortunately, many are not. Local agencies can set their own procedures. Artificial intelligence resources like ChatGPT (https://chat.openai.com/chat) can help you navigate a state's public records law. Telling ChatGPT to "write a request for a police report from Billings, Montana" will give you a decent first draft.

You can also run a Google search, which might produce a website or example of someone else's public records request. You can also call the agency and ask for the records department. They will usually tell you if there's a website you can use, or another way to request records.

Some sites like http://www.Muckrock.com will assist you with government records requests. These sites are helpful in identifying where to send requests and in suggesting model language. Be careful, though: Most sites don't alert you to important deadlines or help with appeals. Some also expect you to post the records you receive on their site, which might not be appropriate depending on the stage of your investigation.

Some places have a statewide public records request portal. For example, Utah has a Government Records Access and Management Act ("GRAMA") portal. WARNING: Portals are tricky. For example, agencies might click a button that says they will respond "Outside [the] Portal." Then you never hear from them. Consider making a request directly through the agency's website or sending a certified letter.

Not every agency provides an online request method. Some still require snail mail. And sometimes it's better to make the request in person; you can get help on the spot.

Some agencies make you say why you want the records. This is improper – if it's a public record, you're entitled to it regardless of your motive. However, it might not be worth arguing about. We usually give a generic explanation along the lines of "We are looking into this case," or "We are interested in these records." You want to be vague anyway; remember that your request itself is now a public record.

Some agencies require that the request be made in the name of an individual even if it's on behalf of an organization. Some also demand a driver's license or other ID. This is also questionable, but agencies can argue that the requester's identity must be verified because there is usually a limit on the number or frequency of requests. Again, it might not be worth an argument.

What do I say when I'm requesting records?

No specific wording is required. We've seen requests that are pages long (written by a lawyer, usually). We've seen some that are only a few sentences.

Requests should start broad but then get narrower. Thus, we might request "all documents and audiovisual material relating to the death of Renee Clark on or around

What if the case is closed?

It's much easier to get records when your case is considered closed. All states require more disclosure in closed cases.

That's why it's critical that you submit your request for records *before* you do anything to make officials dust off the case. You can hold your press conference or post your "Justice For" page *after* you get the records.

December 2, 1989. This request includes, but is not limited to, reports, witness interviews or statements, transcripts, notes, evidence logs, photographs, audio and visual recordings, forensic testing results, findings, conclusions, summaries of witness testimony, notes, memos, and correspondence. Our request includes all material created or maintained by this agency." If the agency says your request is too broad, you can ask for clarification or narrow it.

Include the case number if you have it (it'll save time). If you're asked for a date range, start the day before the death or disappearance and go through the date of your request.

Depending on the circumstances, we might indicate if we are requesting records on behalf of family, or for our student clinic or a class that we teach. Whether mentioning that you are a podcaster is helpful depends on the agency.

Will you have to pay for the records?

Probably. All states let agencies charge for answering records requests. Common costs include staff time for locating, redacting, and copying/scanning the records.

There are controls on how much you can be charged. For example, most states limit staff charges to the lowest-paid employee qualified to do the work. If the services can be performed by a clerk (usually the case), you might want to object if you're being charged $50 per hour.

If a case file is huge, an agency might claim that going through each document is too time-consuming. The burden of proving that is on the agency, and you must be given a chance to narrow your request.

If you're not trying to make money from your investigation, request a fee waiver. Most states encourage agencies to reduce fees if the request is for a non-commercial purpose, is in the public interest, or other good cause.

How do agencies respond to records requests?

Agencies respond in various ways. They might send the records. They might ignore the request (sadly common with local agencies). They might give you some records and tell you what has been withheld. They might give you some records and *not* tell you what was withheld, or even that anything *was* withheld.

Sometimes you'll receive records with extensive redaction (covered sections). For example:

Agencies do have to redact some information, one obvious example being social security numbers. But they frequently over-redact. For example, names of governmental employees are nearly always public. In some states, witnesses' names are too. Yet this information is often covered. Improper redactions may be intentional, or just because the records clerk has not received updated training.

I've received no response, incomplete response, over-redacted response, or a denial. Now what?

In many cases, you will need to consider an appeal. You *have* to appeal if you don't hear back – you can't just send a reminder or follow up request, or you might have waived your right to insist on the records. We've seen agencies simply adopt blanket policies of not fulfilling any requests. Sometimes, a records clerk receives limited (or no) training.

A public records appeal isn't like a court appeal. It's a written appeal that you submit to the records official's supervisor, town council, etc. In more populated areas, record appeals might go to a committee.

How do you know where to send it? The agency is supposed to tell you where and how to appeal when they respond to your original request. Unfortunately, many aren't that helpful. They'll provide a response without a cover letter, without any information about appealing, or not respond at all.

You could call the agency and ask how to appeal but take what it says with a grain of salt. You might find information through internet research. For example, we might run a Google search for Texas +public records +appeal or Nebraska +appeal +records +denial.

Expect 2 or more levels of appeal. In most states, if you remain dissatisfied after that process, you can file a court action. You can do all of this without an attorney, although it's easier if a lawyer or paralegal will help you.

What do I say in an appeal?

No particular wording is required for an appeal. It can be a few sentences. Depending on the circumstances you might write something like, "I did not receive any response to my public records request. I am appealing this denial. Because the agency did not provide any reasons for denying the request, it is my understanding that the agency has waived any arguments against giving me the records."

If the response was incomplete and no explanation was given, the appeal might be as simple as identifying missing material that should have been provided. You might write something like, "I was only given the typed reports. I believe the audio and videos are also public records and should also been provided." Or "My request included a copy of the evidence logs in this case. These logs are public records and should be provided."

NOTE: If you see records mentioned that weren't provided with a response, you might try a new request rather than (or in addition to) an appeal. Your new request can say something like, "We previously requested and received police reports for this case. In the reports, we saw a reference to photographs (etc.) We are now requesting all photographs in the file."

If the response was incomplete and you were given an explanation, your appeal will need to address the reason(s) you were given. In many cases, the reason will be that the case is still active or open. Your appeal might be a challenge to whether the case really was active. You might request proof of the last time it had been worked *before the agency received your records request.* In 2017, the Arkansas Supreme Court upheld an order releasing records of a 1963 murder where activity on the case was "sparse" before a 2014 records request.

You might also argue that you are entitled to some documents even if the case is open, as discussed above. Depending on the circumstances, you might write something like, "You have advised me that this case is being actively worked. I believe I am still entitled to initial incident reports, 911 calls, body camera footage, and other public records even if the case is open."

In some cases, you can write a list of information about the case that the agency has given to the media, arguing that this information has been publicly disclosed and can't be withheld now. If you want to play hardball and you learn that police have presented a case to outside organizations (such as The Vidocq Society or the American Investigative Society of Cold Cases (AISOCC)), you can argue that this is a disclosure and the agency cannot discriminate among private recipients in sharing information.

Some appeals can be pages long, with statutes and cases. ChatGPT can help. Telling ChatGPT to "write an appeal from denial of public records in Arkansas" (or other location) produces a decent template. You still have to fill in case-specific information, of course.

If you're hard core, you can search Google scholar (http://www.scholar.Google.com) for cases where a public records response was appealed. You can dig up the underlying court case online or by contacting the clerk. The exhibits will usually include the original request, the response, and any appeal, which you can use as examples.

What's my deadline to appeal?

It depends on the state. The agency is supposed to tell you, but they often don't. It's not hard to find on Google, for example, by searching [state] +public records +appeal +deadline.

What if you don't get a response? You can't just send reminder emails or re-submit the same request; the agency can argue that your remedy for nondisclosure was an appeal and you didn't pursue one. Once the agency's deadline for responding has passed, your appeal clock is ticking. It works like this: You submit your request. Let's say that state law gives an agency 3 business days to respond to the request, then gives you 14 calendar days to appeal an unsatisfactory response. Three business days have gone by with no response. Under state law, starting on Day 4, you now have two weeks to submit an appeal. Calendaring these dates is critical, so the agency can't claim your appeal was too late. (We've made that mistake ourselves in the past.)

Some appeal procedures seem intended to discourage appeals. For example, some places won't accept appeals by email, even if receipt can be confirmed. But stick with it!

Can I appeal the fees?

Yes. Fees must be reasonable. If an agency says it will cost $400 to respond to a request, request a detailed explanation. Ask for ways to reduce the cost. Ask what is being charged for staff time. Ask to view the records instead of having the whole file copied. (This is sometimes not allowed because information in original documents doesn't have redactions required by state law. Some will let you view the documents – without taking any notes or pictures – and then redact those for which you request copies.)

Mug shots

Mug shots are government records and quite helpful. Not only do they show what a person looked like at a point in time, but they usually include a physical description, aliases, tattoos, why the person was arrested, etc.

A growing number of states limit disclosure of mug shots unless a person has been convicted. (That makes sense. In many cases, charges are dropped or never brought. Arrestees are also presumed innocent until convicted.)

Mugshots.com used to offer millions of mug shots but has been hobbled by legal issues. You can try Googling mug shot +[state/county]. Some county jails post their current inmate roster with photos. If you need an older mug shot, it can be obtained through a public records request to the arresting agency. The request can be as simple as, "I am requesting a copy of all mug shots for Jana Porter, date of birth xx-xx-xxxx," or "Emily Stevenson, who was in your jail at some point between 1983 and 1992."

Federal records

Disclosure of federal records is governed by the Freedom of Information Act ("FOIA"). Each agency has a FOIA portal. For example, FBI records are requested through https://efoia.fbi.gov. Drug Enforcement Administration records are requested at https://www.dea.gov/foia.

The FOIA system is broken. It's good at telling you if an agency does *not* have records – that bad news usually comes within a few weeks. For whatever reasons (budget, staffing, lack of accountability), if a federal agency *does* have records, it can be months – or years – before you get them. Suing the agency might speed up the process, but it requires resources the average Joe or Jane doesn't have.

Federal agencies sometimes post FOIA responses online. For example, a search on the Nuclear Regulatory Commission's FOIA page, http://www.nrc.gov/reading-rm/foia will show documents produced regarding the mysterious 1974 death of Karen Silkwood in Oklahoma.

The FBI's "Vault" has FOIA responses from the Atlanta Child Murders, the Zodiac Killer, Jeffrey Dahmer, Olivia Newton-John (yes, really), and other individuals or cases of public interest. It's of limited value in most cold cases, but it doesn't hurt to search. https://vault.fbi.gov/.

Was your subject a truck driver? Consider requesting documents from the Department of Transportation, https://www.transportation.gov/foia. The Social Security Administration, https://www.ssa.gov/foia/request.html, will provide summaries of death claims. Look for federal ties to your person of interest and what records might be available.

Other sources of records

Was your victim stabbed on a city bus? Consider the local transit authority. Were EMTs called? Consider the fire department. Was 911 called? Check to see who provides dispatch services. NOTE: Some tribal agencies do not have established provisions for requesting records. It might require family involvement. If the case you are investigating occurred in or near an Indian reservation and you can't find records, double-check boundaries. Many states have pockets of federal jurisdiction because (for example) a site is, or used to be, part of a reservation or other tribal land.

NON-GOVERNMENTAL RECORDS

Most private companies will not give you records if you're not on the account. Perhaps a naïve or friendly employee will look something up for you, especially if you ask in person or through a mutual acquaintance. (*See* our Risks of Working Cold Cases section for when you can use documents improperly given to you.)

Releases might help. If you are, or know, a family member or the personal representative of the victim's estate, and if they're already aware of your investigation, ask them to sign an authorization to release records. You should also have anyone who requested the investigation sign a similar release if their movements or actions have not been verified.

Most people will not sign general releases allowing you unfettered access to documents. You should specify what you will be requesting, such as, "I authorize… to request and obtain all records associated with [Victim's/my] cellular account XXX and my cellular number xxx-xxx-xxxx from January 1, 2013 through June 1, 2013."

Unless a company requires you to use a specific format, no particular wording is required. You can run a search on ChatGPT like "draft an authorization to release bank records" and it will spit out something you can adapt.

SOCIAL MEDIA RESEARCH

Social media is invaluable to an investigator. Facebook, Instagram, Twitter, Pinterest, TikTok, etc., make locating individuals and analyzing their lives easier than ever.

One use of social media is to investigate people. Locating a person's page/account might be as simple as going to the platform and searching for the person's name (especially if it's uncommon). Or checking known acquaintances' pages and seeing if your person is listed as a friend. Your subject might comment on his mother's photo, or wish a friend a happy birthday. "People search" sites like Truthfinder.com sometimes have this information as well.

Some people prefer to search social media using a pseudonym (fake account), particularly if researching a person of interest. Either way, we start by reviewing the subject's entire page. We note friends, regular commenters, mentions of jobs, birthdays, relationships, etc. We check every item under "About" columns. We check the Facebook page URL, which can include middle initials or names, birth names, former married names, etc. It also appears that persons of interest seem more likely to have multiple Facebook pages; consider that some might be under aliases.

We then review the other individuals' pages, looking for comments, descriptions of events or disputes, expressions of sympathy, etc. In one case, a soon-to-be ex-husband decided to air grievances publicly at the time of a divorce – including references to how his wife had hurt our victim. The wife reminded him that his comments were public, but he left them up for us to see 9 years later. In another case, a missing person had a vague exchange on a friend's page the day before he went missing, ending with the friend's odd comment, "I hope you know what you're doing."

Social media search techniques change frequently. We recommend OSINT (Open Source Intelligence) books and resources for the latest search techniques on social media platform(s). For example, a search for "How to search Facebook comments" on Reddit.com produces a number of tutorials. The website http://www.OSINTframework.com has helpful links free online resources for tracing usernames, email addresses, IP addresses, etc.

NOTE: If you're not familiar with a social media platform, check with someone who is. For example, some sites will notify accountholders if you attempt to take a screen shot.

COURT RECORDS RESEARCH

Court records are a great source in cold cases. It might surprise some to learn that most court files – including warrants on open cases – are public. We can thank the "Star Chamber" of old England. It was so hated for secretive court proceedings and abuse of basic rights that the framers of our Constitution went to great lengths to make judicial proceedings and court orders public.

There are a few exemptions, such as juvenile matters and adoptions. Until recently, even most divorce files were public. (The final decree itself is usually public because it is a court order.) Grand jury proceedings are secret.[3]

---

[3] One notable exception is the JonBenet Ramsey case. In that case, a court unsealed part of a grand jury proceeding after some jurors publicly contradicted statements of the district attorney.

How are court records helpful?

Court records can give you birth dates, middle names, residences, the names of employers and persons who provided personal guarantees of the defendant's appearance, etc. They can reveal motives, fill in timelines, show a history of violence, etc. As Coalition cofounder Jason Jensen says, our biggest advantage over earlier investigators is the passage of time: We know whether a suspect was later convicted of similar crimes, or lived an uneventful life.

In many cold cases, victims, witnesses, or suspects/persons of interest have been involved in court cases. The victim might have been mid-divorce. Or a person of interest might have been charged in connection with your subject's death, but the charges were later dropped. Some potentially useful information we've gotten from court records include:

- Suspect D was charged with murder of Victim E. However, he was also suspected of 3 other unsolved murders. The court case involving Victim E contains extensive discussion of the other victims' cases.

- Husband died from drinking antifreeze while at a remote location with new Wife. Bankruptcy court records revealed that Wife was in dire financial straits that were conveniently resolved by Husband's death. The clerk's notes in a probate court proceeding contain a statement (not found anywhere else) that the county attorney suspects Wife's involvement in the death.

- Missing Person A's mother believed that A was secretly cooperating with law enforcement in investigations. This is not an uncommon belief (hope) by parents. However, a careful review of A's court records revealed an intriguing new pattern of arrest-and-release shortly before her death...

- Missing Person J was in a heated divorce with Wife when he disappeared. Wife claimed he had decided to reconcile. Court records confirmed that Husband was not moving forward with the divorce.

- In a medical malpractice lawsuit, B's husband testified that B once stuck a gun in his ribs. This might (or might not) be enlightening when B is later suspected of shooting someone at close range.

- Suspect P was convicted of violating the Mann Act (sex trafficking). The court record includes comments made by a co-worker about P's suspected involvement in the unsolved death of his wife.

- Wayne B. Williams was suspected of more than 20 murders in Atlanta from 1979-81. He was only charged in the deaths of two teenagers, but prosecutors were allowed to introduce evidence of 10 other murders of which they suspected him. For this reason, Wayne Williams' court file has information about numerous homicides.

- In a 2003 case, it was "undetermined" how a woman was shot in the head while with her boyfriend. But we found these enlightening notes about the boyfriend in a court case filed a few days earlier when his mother asked for a protective order:

```
06-23-2003   **** PRIVATE **** Filed: Ex Parte Motion to Dismiss Protective
             Order.
06-24-2003   **** PRIVATE **** Filed: ORDER TO DISMISS EX PARTE DENIED ON
             6/23/03 BY RSD
06-24-2003   Note: DENIED. MS NEILSON CAME IN WITH SOME YOUNG LADY WHO
             APPEARED TO BE ENCOURAGING HER TO DROP THIS.  HER SON IS IN
             JAIL NOW ON SOME OTHER CHARGES.  STABBING A FEW YEARS AGO.
             COURT DENIED DISMISSAL AND DIRECTED HER TO APPEAR AT HEARING ON
             6/25/03 TO
06-24-2003   Note: DISCUSS WITH COMMISSIONER.  APPEARS SONS IS STILL TRYING
             TO CONTROL HER.  SHE IS FRIGHTENED OF HIM BUT APPEARS TO BE A
             CARETAKER.  RECOMMENED NO DISMISSAL. RSD
```

State criminal / court records

Availability of court records differs from state to state and even within states. Consider starting with http://www.JudyRecords.com, which compiles free public court records from numerous states.

Finding court records can be as simple as running a Google search. Suppose you saw in a news article that a person of interest in your case was arrested in Dallas. To see what is available online, you can start with a simple search, Dallas +"criminal records". That produces this site: https://www.dallascounty.org/services/record-search/. Searching is free; the records themselves have a cost.

What records are available? It depends on the state. Most states offer criminal histories for employers to run background checks on job applicants. Some examples:

- Florida: The Florida Department of Law Enforcement has a criminal history site that goes back decades. https://www.fdle.state.fl.us/Criminal-History-Records/Record-Check\. Searches are $24; the results (if any) are emailed to you.

- Montana: The Montana Division of Criminal Investigation offers criminal background searches for $20. https://doj.egovmt.com/choprs/

These sites typically don't have the court records themselves. For that, you might need to search for [location] +"court records". Some state court systems let you conduct statewide searches. Random examples:

- Missouri: The Missouri Courts page allows statewide searches back to the 1990s. https://www.courts.mo.gov/cnet/nameSearch.do?newSearch=Y

- Utah: "Xchange" lets anyone search statewide. https://xchange.utcourts.gov/XchangeWEB/XchangeWebServlet. Court dockets *(indexes of documents filed in the case)* are available from the mid-1980s. The documents themselves are available beginning in the 2010s, or occasionally earlier.

- Wisconsin: Wisconsin Circuit Court access allows statewide searches: https://wcca.wicourts.gov/

- King County, Washington: You can search cases for free, but must pay to see documents. https://dja-prd-ecexap1.kingcounty.gov/?q=node/501

In some states, you have to conduct a separate search for each court location. That is why you might want to start with the general criminal history search; it can save you time by telling you which court(s) are more likely to have records on your subject.

NOTE: Most online court systems require you to register. If court records are not available online, they can be requested by phone or email or in person. Court clerks are usually quite helpful. Expect to pay a fee for retrieval and copying of the records.

Warrants

The Fourth Amendment generally prohibits warrantless searches and seizures by the government. The drafters of our constitution didn't want people arrested without "probable cause." Officers wanting an arrest warrant submit affidavits laying out facts they believe show probable cause. If a judge agrees, the warrant is issued. If there's no time for a warrant, officers submit an "affidavit of probable cause" after a warrantless arrest.

The same process applies to searches. Even when someone is arrested, a warrant must usually be obtained to search items (like a cell phone or backpack) in her possession.

Warrants and probable cause statements are gold mines. They usually aren't redacted; all the juicy details are there to see. They're also detailed, because police don't want them challenged by defense attorneys. (If a search is later found to have been conducted without probable cause, evidence might be excluded from use at trial.)

Because warrants are court orders, they must be made public within a short time after they are executed, even if the case is still open. For that reason, some courts make search warrants difficult to find before charges have been filed. (By contrast, open *arrest* warrants are more widely available, to encourage people to check for outstanding warrants. Search Google for [state] +warrants.)

If you can't figure out how to search for warrants on a court's website, call and ask the clerk. They will usually tell you and might even look it up for you. It's still hard, though – in many jurisdictions, warrants can't be searched by subject name. Perhaps you can narrow your search to a particular date, agency, or detective, but you could be clicking on a lot of irrelevant warrants to find the one(s) you want, incurring a charge every time you click. You can request a copy from the court, but you'll probably need the same information (date, officer, etc.) for them to find it.

Federal court records

Federal court records can be located in a couple of ways. You might want to start with Google Scholar, discussed more below. It has some many federal trial court rulings (but very few state trial court rulings). Also check the federal court website PACER. Its case locator, https://pcl.uscourts.gov/pcl/index.jsf, will let you search cases nationwide from the early '90s. (It's also worth checking for earlier cases. Sometimes older documents are uploaded if they become relevant later on. For example, a defendant might file a motion for new trial in 2018 with exhibits from his case that was closed decades earlier.)

Court documents weren't posted on PACER until the mid-2000s. But PACER will show you a Docket (a list of filings in the case in chronological order) in cases from the 1980s.

If you need older court documents, call or email the records clerk at the courthouse where the case was. It's expensive. Federal courts can charge $65 just to look for the case. Be prepared to pay $.50 per page for copies. We once spent $410 on copies from one federal case (but worth it).

You should search federal cases even if you think your subject was never arrested by the feds. State prisoners sometimes file lawsuits in federal court seeking a "writ of habeas corpus," arguing that they should be released because their *state* court conviction or sentence violated the *federal* constitution. Parts of the state court proceeding will be quoted or attached to the federal court filings.

Virtual court hearings

When COVID-19 struck in 2020, courts began holding hearings online, using applications like Webex or Zoom. Members of the general public could now watch ordinary proceedings without having to go to the courthouse, and without having their presence known to the defendant. (Public watchers can usually sign on anonymously.) Many courts have continued this practice.

How is that helpful in cold cases? In one case, we attempted surveillance at a restaurant where a person of interest from an old case was said to work. Unfortunately, we had no idea what she looked like. While running a routine court search for this individual, we found she had recently been arrested on unrelated charges, and an upcoming virtual hearing was scheduled. Criminal defendants are required to attend most proceedings even if they don't want to. We logged in to watch, and now we know exactly what she looks like.

Appeals and appellate documents

An appeal can be taken by any party to a criminal or non-criminal (civil) case. Appeals are helpful in a couple of ways. First, the court's ruling might have helpful information. More important, people involved in appeals have to file "briefs", discussed below.

How do you know if someone you're interested in was involved in an appeal? A great site is Google Scholar, http://scholar.google.com, which has decades of appellate court rulings from throughout the United States. On the site, click the "case law" option, and start searching. (Don't limit your search to federal or a particular state unless you're certain your subject never had a criminal conviction anywhere else.) It's a Google site, so the search tools are the same. Options on the left side of the page let you narrow your search to specific courts, areas, or date ranges.

You can also check the court docket of the original court case. The docket will show if an appeal was filed but didn't end up with a ruling, perhaps because it was dismissed due to a settlement or a violation of court rules.

Other sites can be used to search for appeals. Westlaw and Lexis are pay sites. They're expensive but are sometimes available for free at local courthouses or law libraries.

Appellate briefs. As mentioned above, parties involved in an appeal have to file "briefs". Contrary to their name, these filings are much longer than the court's ruling. A typical appellate brief might be 30+ pages long with 30+ pages of exhibits; the ruling itself might be only 5 pages. Appellate briefs often contain information that can't be found elsewhere.

Most appellate briefs can be accessed through pay services such as Westlaw or Lexis. Copies are also available at states' highest courts and sometimes at universities. You can learn how to get briefs by calling any state appeals court. Finding an appeals court is as simple as searching Google for [state] +appeals court.

Some real-world examples of appellate briefs that had interesting information relevant to cold cases include:

- Suspect D's murder case file disappeared from the local courthouse. However, before then the government appealed a ruling excluding some evidence. The government's briefs attached hundreds of pages from the court file that later went missing.

- Man was injured in a railyard that happened to be the site of a recent murder. He sued the railroad. The appellate briefs included diagrams of the railyard and the names of several potential witnesses who regularly hung out there.

- Victim's girlfriend T appealed a conviction for drug possession. Her briefs revealed that police saw the drugs after being called to her house because her boyfriend had just been murdered. The briefs discuss how the murder happened, what T saw, etc.

- The mother of Missing Person D remembered some of D's associates, including K. Appellate briefs filed after K's conviction on unrelated charges included a detailed summary of K's criminal activities and gun ownership during the time that D went missing.

- A freight train rider committed similar crimes in three different states in the '80s. We would not have known this except that he appealed his convictions in each of those cases. From those, we were able to include him as a possible suspect in a similar case.

PRISON, PAROLE, EXTRADITION RECORDS

Many persons suspected of involvement in a cold case have been incarcerated. Related records can be helpful.

Prison and jail records

Incarceration histories are public record. They can confirm a suspect's alibi or help complete a timeline.

Legal Status Description	Legal Status Change
DISCHARGED	DISCHARGED/HOLD
INMATE	PAROLE REVOKED
PAROLE VIOLATION	RET PRSN/REV PEND
PAROLE	PAROLE CONTINUED
PAROLE	PAROLE TO CUSTODY
INMATE	NEW COMMITMENT
UNSENTENCED	NEW REFERRAL
DISCHARGED	DISCHARGED/INMATE CASE
INMATE	PAROLE REVOKED
PAROLE VIOLATION	RET PRSN/REV PEND
PAROLE	DISCHARGED/INMATE CASE
COMPACT IN INMATE	COMPACT IN START
PAROLE	PAROLE TO CUSTODY
INMATE	NEW COMMITMENT
UNSENTENCED	NEW REFERRAL
DISCHARGED	DISCHARGED/INMATE CASE
INMATE	PAROLE REVOKED
PAROLE VIOLATION	RET PRSN/REV PEND
PAROLE	PAROLE

Example of actual prison chronology for a suspect

Hearing your victim or suspect

Parole hearings are preserved for years, even decades. They're an opportunity to hear the voice of a now-dead suspect, victim, or witness. It personalizes your victim and adds layers to others.

In one case, prison records had been stuffed in a box and never unpacked. As we went through them, we realized that several people who showed up years later in a triple murder had served time together in the same cell block.

For modern records, you'll probably have to request them from the agency that runs the jail (usually a county sheriff) or prison (usually a department of corrections). Older records might be at an archive, as discussed below.

Parole records

There is no parole for persons convicted in federal court after November 1, 1987. All states have parole systems.

Parole records are partially available. Sensitive documents like victim statements are private. But hearings are otherwise public and can be a wealth of information. In deciding whether a prisoner remains a danger to society, hearing officers might ask not just about the crime of conviction, but others of which he is suspected or was arrested (but not convicted) in the past.

One parole hearing we listened to was chilling. In trying to persuade the parole board that he was not a danger to society, the prisoner described his version of the murder for which he had been convicted. He was then asked about a woman's murder in California of which he was suspected. He chuckled.

Like other prison-related records, the location of parole records depends on their age. They will likely be at either your state's parole agency or a state archive. Search terms might include [state] +parole records.

Extradition records and pardons

A person arrested in one state might refuse to voluntarily return to another state that wants to prosecute her. The state that wants to prosecute can initiate "extradition". Both the state where the person is in custody and the demanding state will have extradition files. These files are public and often contain photographs, fingerprints, criminal histories, and a description of suspected crimes. Depending on their age, they will either be at the office of the governor or secretary of state, or at a state archive.

States and the federal Department of Justice also keep copies of applications for pardons, whether they are granted or denied. These applications include information not just about the crime of conviction, but other aspects of the applicant's criminal history.

MISCELLANEOUS RESOURCES

Genealogy (non-DNA). Relatives are a wealth of information. A family member's murder, disappearance, or witnessing of a crime are stories likely to be passed down. We build family trees for victims, suspects, witnesses, etc. While the most private method is to build trees in an offline program, many people use sites like Ancestry.com, MyHeritage.com, etc. NOTE: Some sites' Terms of Service (TOS) prohibit the use of their services for law enforcement purposes. If you're not law enforcement nor working for law enforcement, you should be good.

Other cases from the same time/area. We commonly request records from solved (closed) murders from the same period. They're easier to get, and they often mention other cases. Detectives from different agencies frequently discussed whether their

Caution!

A note about the popular tree-building site Ancestry.com: Don't use your own tree; start one with an unrevealing name. Change your tree settings to unsearchable and private, and wait 30 days before adding data. Opt out of having others view your visits to their trees. Don't save photos to your tree directly from another tree.

cases might be linked, mentioning similarities and differences. If someone was considered a potential suspect in a similar murder, it might be worth checking him out in your case. We review criminal histories of everyone named in both cases.

Medical Examiner records. M.E. records and autopsies are governed by separate laws. In a few states, they're not available at all. In others, they are semi-public or can be requested by family. Try a simple Google search like "autopsy report" with your state name or ask ChatGPT to write a request for an autopsy report from your state/county.

Death records. Access to modern death records is usually limited to family, estate representatives, etc. Indexes might be available, and some states like Kentucky, Missouri, and Utah post the actual documents after 50 years. Funeral homes will give a copy to immediate family. They're also filed in probate cases. If your subject owned real estate, check property records; death certificates were often filed when a victim's real property was sold.[4]

Unclaimed property. Check http://www.MissingMoney.com or your state's unclaimed property website. When people die or vanish, their affairs are not in order. Many end up being owed money. Someone might pay car insurance but become entitled to a refund if the car is sold after his disappearance. Or have money in a bank account. Or is owed a final paycheck. This unclaimed money eventually is reported to the state. If that happens, consider submitting a records request to the state

---

[4] Many county recorders have searchable websites for property records. Some require a subscription, but many allow free searches and only charge when a copy is requested. Or you can go in person, or call the recorder and ask if they'll do a search.

treasurer's office. The file might include information about efforts that were made to locate the owner (your victim).

Corporate records. Consider checking the history and ownership of businesses that feature in your case. Some state department of commerce sites also allow you to search by owner name, which could be revealing (if, for example, a subject co-owned a business with a witness). In one of our cases, we submitted a public records request and learned that our suspect had been denied a casino license in the 1970s because of his "extensive criminal history."

City directories. Ancestry.com, local libraries, and others have excellent collections of city directories. City directories are helpful in identifying neighbors, local businesses, and cross streets.

Vertical files. This is an old-fashioned term for material compiled by libraries on different subjects or family names. In one Kentucky library, a single volunteer had extracted and indexed thousands of death notices and local interest stories from a newspaper that is still not available online.

Yearbooks. Ancestry.com and Classmates.com have great yearbook collections. These can identify classmates to be interviewed, and sometimes provide the only photograph of a victim or suspect at a certain age.

License plate readers. License plate readers can be very helpful in tracing a subject's movements. Originally intended to help lenders with repossessions, automated plate readers capture an alarming number of images in many areas over long periods of time. These photos can be accessed through services like TLOxp that usually require a subscription and proof of eligibility to use them (such as a private investigator's license or legal employment). Other license plate information is also available but regulated. See, for example, https://infotracer.com/plate-lookup/ or http://www.bumper.com.

Trackers and other surveillance. In most states, it is illegal for private citizens to place trackers on a car without consent. Police can't use trackers without a warrant. Private investigators might (depending on the state). We've used trackers in urgent situations, as when we heard that a subject was about to flee. In-person surveillance is risky unless you are trained. We leave these things to our PI volunteers.

Building permits / developer / real estate sites. Did your suspect build a shed shortly after his wife disappeared? Building permits might be interesting to check. If a murder occurred in a development/subdivision, sometimes the developer or homebuilder's site will show the layout.

Metal detectors and ground-penetrating radar. Do you think someone buried a body in his yard or under a basement floor? Most homeowners won't let you just start digging, and police can't without probable cause. Ground penetrating radar might be the answer. While metal detectors look for metallic objects, GPR looks for changes in density (like air pockets) that could indicate that the ground has been disturbed. The equipment is expensive, but a local contractor or utility-locating company might rent it or even lend an employee.

A Cold Case Coalition executive team member looking for an unmarked grave using our ground penetrating radar

Aerial photos. Esri's World Imagery Wayback Archive, Google Earth Pro, and other sites offer dated aerial photos. Apart from the fact that they occasionally capture interesting images, they're helpful in seeing what property looked like. In investigating one 1970s case, aerial photos helped us realize just how near other bodies had been found, which we couldn't tell from police sketches.

Archives

Government archives hold older government records – court, law enforcement, prison, land, mug shots, etc. They're often not digitized but detailed descriptions are provided. Some archives will do limited lookups. One sent us a document that had been written by our suspect (referring to himself as the "Petitioner"):

3. Petitioner was given an Immunity Agreement in writting by the District Attorney's Office in and for Weber County. This Document gave Petitioner Immunity from Prosecution for Crimes in the District of Weber County. It is in the Form of a written and legal Document agreed to and signed for Petitioner by his then Counsel and by Assistant Attorney for the County of Weber (approved by the District Attorney Dale Stratford). In violation of the terms of this Immunity agreement Petitioner was Arrested, Prosecuted, Convicted, and Sentenced to Imprisonment, in violation of the Equal Protection Clause of the 14th Amendment to the Constitution of the United States.

This was intriguing because rumor was that this man had ratted out some mobsters. It's vague, but it could suggest he had been granted immunity for some reason…

In another case, we found financial records for a man who had disappeared. This was critical information because some people theorized that he took off due to financial distress. The archival records disproved it; a court-appointed receiver wrote that selling just one of his assets would have covered all of his debt.

Special collections

Most colleges and universities have special collections. They want unique material so you never know what might be there. But interesting things we have found include:

- *Mayors' papers.* One mayor donated papers that included two boxes of material about unsolved murders from the 1980s. Another mayor's papers had a letter from a local diplomat outraged at being questioned about his employee's unsolved murder. The letter contained information about an event they both attended the night of her disappearance.

- *Judges' papers.* One judge's papers included letters from convicted murderers throughout the U.S. describing – in their own words – their cases.

- *Authors' papers.* In one exciting find, we made a list of journalists known to have interviewed a suspected serial killer, then checked whether any of them had donated their papers to a college. We hit paydirt: One author had – and it included a long, never-published interview with new information from the murderer.

- *Organization papers.* While researching the death of a gay man, we learned that a local LGBTQIA+ organization had donated its papers from that era. We didn't find anything on our victim, but we did find things like a note from a prosecutor describing a local killer believed to be targeting gay men.

- *Oral histories.* We wanted to hear what a suspect sounded like. Twenty years earlier, she had interviewed a senior citizen for a local organization. The recording had been donated to a university, which copied it for us. The suspect's husband had been interviewed for a history of mining; that audio (at a different university) included a timeline of where he and the suspect had lived.

- *Photos.* One special collection had scrapbooks from a local sheriff's office. They included original Polaroid pictures of the search for a woman whose body has never been found.

- *Company records.* Libraries occasionally end up with records from large or local companies. These collections typically predate modern privacy laws, so personal information is there to see if you're lucky.

Museums

Museum workers might be historians or longtime residents. One museum director arranged for "old-timers" to come down and talk about a case. We learned a lot, including that none of them had ever been interviewed (even one who lived two doors away from the crime scene).

In another case, we wondered whether a suspect would have had enough time to get to the victim's home from where he dropped off a witness. Reconstructing the drive, we brought along a local museum director. She showed us the most likely route – not what we originally thought.

SECTION V

PUTTING TOGETHER THE CASE

You've gathered information from the internet, newspapers, police reports, court records, etc. The next step is organizing and evaluating what you've got.

ORGANIZING THE INFORMATION

Scanning / copying. We recommend scanning any hard copies that you have. Use a copier or other scanning device that will "OCR" the pages, making them searchable. If you don't have access to such a copier, some libraries no longer charge for scanning. Copy businesses have OCR capabilities. Working from a copy will allow you to highlight and make notes.

Document database. You don't need to use a file organizing app or program, but it can be helpful. One program we use is Evernote. It helps us track a case, allows team members to add and see uploads, and lets us run searches across all of our files. If you have a Gmail account, Google Drive also works well. You can create a folder in your Google Drive and upload any document, image, spreadsheet, etc. If you're familiar with them, you can add a personalized Google MyMaps, a "drawing" canvas (like Lucidchart) for charting information, etc. Each item you add there will have a URL, so you can link to a specific photo, search warrant PDF, etc., in your overall timeline or typed case notes. You can also create subfolders to organize information such as "Police reports,"

"Media," "Witness Interviews," "Crime Scene Photos," etc. Airtable users can upload documents, images, files, etc., directly to your Airtable timeline.

Pagination. We often use a PDF program or scanner to add page numbers to a working copy. Page numbering makes it easier to discuss large files with someone.

Sections. We sometimes sort large files by categories like Reports, Medical Examiner/Autopsy Reports, Witness Statements, Evidence Logs, Court Documents, Pre-Disappearance Documents, Family Information, etc. The Los Angeles Police Department Murder Book, https://www.ojp.gov/ncjrs/virtual-library/abstracts/homicide-investigation-case-file-profile-los-angeles-police, identifies 18 sections. Several don't apply to civilian investigations, but it is still helpful.

Chronological. Sorting police reports into chronological order can help track the progress of the investigation. It can also spot areas for follow up (for example, witnesses who were mentioned but never contacted). We sometimes do separate chronologies for individual detectives, just to get a better feel for how they viewed the case.

EVALUATING THE INFORMATION

You've organized your information. Now it's time to evaluate it. First, look at the overall impression. How thorough was the original investigation? Did detectives talk to everyone you would expect? Did they develop a theory? Do you believe they missed or misinterpreted anything? Some cold case investigators contend that the perpetrator's name is usually found in the original case file.

Why did the investigation stall out? What information can be updated? Can additional forensic testing be done? Will witnesses be more open now? What do photos suggest?

Prepare to double check everything for which you don't see documentation. In one case we investigated, police found it suspicious that a missing man vanished the day before he had been subpoenaed to testify against his own brother in a felony trial. It sure was – except that it wasn't true. Court officials in San Francisco dug up the 1970s court case for us. The missing man had not been subpoenaed and was never even named as a potential witness. (And the charges were relatively minor, not likely to produce much if any prison time.)

CRIMINAL DOCKET UNITED STATES DISTRICT COURT	CR 75	353 CR	CFP
D. C. Form No. 100 Rev.	CLOSING CARD PREPARED		
TITLE OF CASE		**ATTORNEYS**	
THE UNITED STATES		For U. S.:	
vs.			
ARREOLA, DANIEL			
SANTI, ALBERT			
		For Defendant:	
		Barry Portman AFPD	
		for Santi	
18:2314 & 2315 Transport falsely made & counterfeited securities			
18:371 Falsely made & counterfeit certificates of Sunbeam Corp. Stock	3 Counts		

You might not be able to tell from the records whether evidence still exists. Be prepared for a reality we've seen many times: Particularly in pre-2000s cases, our estimate is that evidence is missing in a quarter of cold cases or more. Perhaps it wasn't transferred to a new location due to space concerns. Or it was tossed when a case was erroneously closed. In one police department, an evidence technician was found to have marked for destruction valuable evidence which she then sold.

One important part of reviewing a case with fresh eyes is looking for information that would now be viewed skeptically. It's not fair to criticize earlier generations of law enforcement for not anticipating today's standards, but it's important to be aware of evidence formerly considered persuasive that is now questioned. Some examples:

Witness statements. These can obviously be helpful, especially if made at the time by a disinterested party with time or reason to notice things. But witnesses can be wrong (several studies have demonstrated the (un)reliability of eyewitness testimony). You'll want to compare what a witness says to other evidence. What about statements made decades later? Don't disregard them, but perhaps scrutinize them more closely. Memories fade. People are influenced by things they've heard or read in the meantime.

911 call analysis. Analysis of wording, pauses, and other indicators in 911 calls has been used in up to 1,500 homicide cases to assess potential involvement of the caller. FBI studies in 2020 and 2022 cautioned against relying on such analysis.

Bloodstain pattern analysis. A 2009 report by the Forensic Science Commission warned against largely "subjective" analysis of bloodstain patterns.

Polygraphs. If someone was ruled out because he passed a polygraph or became a focus because she failed or refused one, be cautious. There's a reason that polygraphs are still inadmissible in court 80 years after their first use, and suspects often decline them because they know how fallible they are. NOTE: The FBI is working on a new deception detection method involving eye movement. There is also a type of deception detection called statement analysis, which focuses on a person of interest's wording.

Polygraphs: A cautionary tale

As recounted in Creighton Horton's *A Reluctant Prosecutor*, in 1985 "serial killer Arthur Gary Bishop confessed to kidnapping, sexually abusing, and murdering five young boys between 1979 and 1983, and led police to the victims' bodies. In three of the five cases, the police had concluded prior to Bishop's confession that the victims' parents were somehow responsible for the disappearance of their own children, based on the fact that they had failed polygraph tests administered by the police polygrapher."

Shoe treads. Shoe prints can show size and type of shoe, unusual wear pattern, etc. However, forensic commissions have expressed concern about relying on comparison of similar shoe treads, which is subjective and has not been extensively studied.

Confessions. Confessions are handy but must be scrutinized. False confessions are common. In cases where prisoners have been factually exonerated of murder by DNA, nearly a third had falsely confessed. More than a third of juveniles who have been exonerated by DNA had falsely confessed. In 1996, Angie Dodge was murdered in Idaho Falls, Idaho. Christopher Tapp confessed and was sentenced to life in prison. Years later, Angie's mother Carol watched videotapes of the interrogation. To her horror, she realized that Tapp's confession had been coerced, and that he was probably innocent. Carol began investigating her daughter's murder and teamed up with Tapp's mother urging police to reopen the case. After 17 years in prison, Tapp was released in 2021 when DNA identified the true killer.

Hair comparison. Other than unchangeable qualities like original color, visual hair comparison is largely discredited. In 2015, the FBI concluded that hair-comparison testimony in at least 90% of trials it reviewed overestimated the usefulness of visually comparing strands of hair. (By contrast, *DNA* from hair is very reliable.)

Fiber comparison. "Fiber comparison" can be a red flag. Was it just a visual comparison (comparing the appearance of one fiber to another)? If so, proceed with caution.

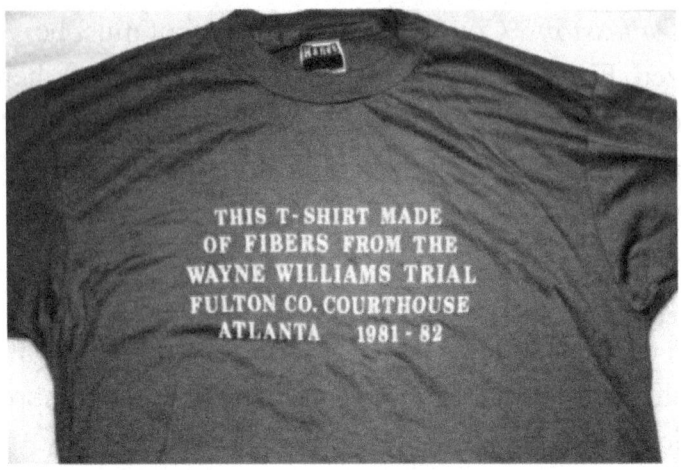

T-shirt commenting (sort of) on fiber evidence that persuaded prosecutors that Wayne B. Williams committed the Atlanta Child Murders.

Bite mark evidence. Debunked. One (in)famous example: Ray Krohn was sentenced to death – twice – by testimony from a forensic dentist about a "snaggletooth" bite mark. Krohn was eventually exonerated by DNA – and the true killer did not even have unusual teeth. See other examples in M. Chris Fabricant, *Junk Science and the American Criminal Justice System* (2022). NOTE: Comparing teeth to an x-ray is sound.

Bullet-bullet comparison. Comparing bullets to each other is helpful when they have distinguishing characteristics like a right-hand twist with six grooves and lands. But other forms of bullet-bullet comparison (like comparing material from unfired bullets) have been discredited. By contrast, comparing a bullet to a *gun* has been studied extensively and is considered solid.

Sketches. Sketches based on witness descriptions can depict skin color, hair color, and eyewear at the time of an incident. See some famous examples at https://www.buzzfeed.com/sarathompson1/bad-police-composite-sketches. But sketches are inherently subjective; someone is drawing based on what someone else is trying to remember and describe. A victim's son once said to us, "I could take 10 photos of you right now and one of them would match that sketch." A compilation of Ted Bundy sketches is available on the internet – some were pretty close; others were way off.

For reasons that are not clear to us, sketches are frequently missing from older case files. If they were hand drawn, there's not much you can do except check with retired detectives, local archives, or perhaps the family of the artist if police had a regular. If the sketch was done with Identi-Kit (developed in 1959), you can recreate it if reports mention the Identi-Kit "code". It will look something like A03 N03 C05 E31 (etc.) (We can recreate it for you if you don't have access to one of the old Identi-Kits.) It is important to look for all sketches that were created in a case. Here's an example of why:

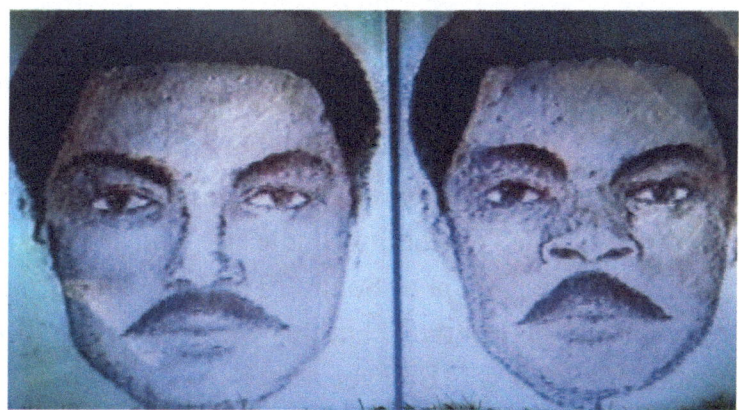

For decades, investigators in Rachael Runyan's murder (1982 Sunset, Utah) looked for a black man based on the sketch on the right. Then Cold Case Coalition cofounder and private detective Jason Jensen found a long-lost earlier sketch *(left)*. Suddenly, Hispanic men were in play.

"Things only the killer would know"

You may see in a file, or be told, that a suspect knew information that "only the killer would know." Be careful. Police might not know the source of the information, and might even have *been* the source of the information.

In 2019, at the request of family we investigated the murder of Marla Scharp (1978 Provo, Utah). The case had been closed by a confession from Henry Lee Lucas, who claimed hundreds of murders in the 1980s. The file indicated that Lucas knew things "only the killer would know." That sounded good – until we listened to the original interviews. They revealed that much of the information had been given to him (by another agency) before the interview, and that Lucas would make repeated guesses until he hit the "right" answer. Some examples:

(Claim) Lucas described the 26-year-old victim. Lucas's initial guess was that 5 people had been killed, then that it was a "little girl".

Lucas described a Budweiser beer tap handle. Lucas was asked if he carried a beer tap handle. He said yes, then guessed it was Blue Ribbon or Schlitz. The interviewer finally said, "I hate to be suggestive… but this was Budweiser." Lucas then "remembered" it was Budweiser.

Lucas described the house. Lucas initially guessed it was a farmhouse (it was actually mid-city).

Lucas knew she had been strangled. Lucas's first guess was that she was stabbed.

Lucas described the crime scene. Lucas was shown photos of the crime scene before describing it.

A suspect might have information from any number of sources. He might receive or guess information from the questioning process. He might simply confirm information he was told. In studying the false confessions of Henry Lee Lucas, we found – throughout the U.S. – instances where he supposedly "knew things only the killer would know," only for the real killer to be revealed by DNA years later. NOTE: Many of these Lucas cases have not yet been reopened.

Evaluating other information

Keep an open mind. Police may believe Deborah Wilde did it, but you're here to provide fresh eyes. There's a reason Debbie wasn't charged in the first place.

Don't believe everything you read. Spoiler alert: People lie. They also jump to conclusions. Mistakes are made. Double-check everything, even statements by law enforcement. (As a former president would say, "Trust but verify.")

Don't believe everything you hear. We've received many tips on our 24/7 Tip Line that a caller's relative (friend, co-worker, neighbor) killed someone. Perhaps he looked like a sketch. Or lived near the victim. Or was later convicted of a sex offense. These reports are usually sincere but unfounded. Of course we follow up.

Don't zero in on one theory / suspect too soon. Some cases are cold because law enforcement got tunnel vision on one theory or suspect. It's human nature; we describe our cofounder's own obsession in *Cold Case Talk: Who Killed Jennie Bowden?*

Examine motives. Although prosecutors aren't required to prove motive, it's helpful to explore it. Was the crime committed out of love, greed, or revenge – who was jealous, who was desperate, who was angry at the decedent? Who would benefit from his death or disappearance? Stranger-on-stranger crimes are rare, but don't rule it out.

SECTION VI

INTERVIEWING

General principles

You've researched the case, organized and evaluated your information, and prepared a timeline. It's time to start reaching out. Some general principles:

Be careful. If you're meeting in person, try a public location, let someone know where you are, and/or consider using a tracking service like Life360.

Try to record if possible. We're usually up front about recording but if that's not feasible, digital voice recorders on sites like Amazon.com work well. Examples include recorders that look like fitness watches, pens, squares that fit in pockets, etc. NOTE: Learn your state's laws about recording without consent. (*See* our Risks of Working Cold Cases section below.) Assume you are also being recorded.[5]

Studies show that conversational, nonconfrontational techniques are effective. Ask open-ended questions. You don't want to suggest answers or reveal your theory. Information you learn might be tainted or unusable in court. You don't have to get creative with your questions, "That's interesting. Why did the family think that?" or "What do you remember about that

---

[5] We upload recordings to an app called Otter (Otter.ai). There's a free version, or for more minutes you can pay a monthly fee. It produces rough but fast and searchable transcripts.

day?" or "What did you do next?" or "What did the police ask you?" are just fine.

Interviewees will ask questions about the case. You probably shouldn't answer most of them and might have to lie. (It's legal, even for police.) You can say you don't remember, you don't have your notes with you, whatever vague mumbling redirects the conversation. When asked who else we've interviewed, we usually indicate that we're not permitted to disclose that information. Also, refrain from committing to any particular course of action; the interviewee might think it's a great idea to go to the media, or the local sheriff, or a particular witness, but it might not be in the best interest of your investigation at that stage.

If you ask about persons of interest, try to do so casually, as though you are just checking off a routine list of people and not for a particular reason. Family members in particular are quick to spread news of a potential suspect. Word might get back to him, or it could taint later interviews.

Interviewing family

Even if you're a member of the family, you should interview other relatives. They might have different information or recollections. They might have talked to different people. Also, family often receive information from people who will not speak with police.

The police (or you) might suspect that a family member was involved in the crime. You should not automatically assume that a family member is uninvolved, even if they asked you to work on the case. (That's a more common deflection technique than some realize.) Treat all family interviews the same and assume they will compare notes. You don't want to give away any suspicions prematurely.

Family members sometimes don't want to discuss a case. That's understandable; you might be tearing open a wound. As you've seen, plenty of other work can be done. If relatives see that you are genuinely trying to resolve the case, it might make them more comfortable. In one case, a victim's brother refused to speak with us because (he told a sibling) "we're just in it for money," even after she noted that we are all volunteers and there is no money. As word got back to him of our progress, especially when police agreed to reopen his sister's case, his attitude changed.

Consider getting to know the interviewee before starting in with questions. Ask about the victim in happier times. What was he like as a brother? What was she like when they met? Did she like reading, sports, dancing? Friendly questions allow fond memories to flow in (we hope).

Ask if they have any photos of the victim, and who else might have some. Ask about other things unrelated to the crime – who were the victim's friends? Coworkers? Did she like her job? What did she do in her spare time? Ease into whether there was anything that might have been worrying her. Ask if she mentioned anything odd happening.

Eventually, you have to ask about the events. There's no right or wrong way. You could say, "I'm sorry, I have to ask you about when Michelle died." They know it's coming. It's sometimes revealing to ask how they first learned about the event. Ask if the family had any theories about what happened.

Did the police? What would the interviewee do next if she were investigating the case?

Interviewing witnesses and acquaintances

Many people have information but don't know how to reach out or won't go to the trouble. When contacted, however, they are happy to talk. Much of the approach is similar, especially if the witness knew the victim. Friends might know a different aspect of the victim's life, for example, whether he was considering divorce, was worried about money or his job, etc.

Start with broad questioning like "Has anyone else asked you about the incident?" "Why were you there?" "What did you hear?" "What did they look like?" Then you can narrow it. For example, if a witness describes a suspect, you can refine her estimates (height, weight, hair, etc.) by asking comparisons to persons known to you both (which might include you): "Was he taller or shorter than your brother Keith? Was his hair darker or lighter than mine?"

There are two schools of thought on showing suspect photos to witnesses. On one hand, if they emphatically say No, you can move on and save time. If they say Yes or are unsure, have you tainted a later identification? Should you put together a photo array (series of photos)? Almost any photo display can be picked apart by a defense attorney – "The men's hair is different length. My client's photo shouldn't have been in the middle. Etc." But it might still be preferable. Or perhaps use a stack, showing one photo at a time and just asking generic questions like, "Do you recognize any of these people?"

Some professionals, such as health care providers or therapists, might refuse to discuss the victim unless – or even if – you are an official representative of the victim's estate. You might be able to get a court order (which the provider might welcome, since many do want to help so long as it is within legal boundaries).

NOTE: If an informant reaches out, respond as quickly as possible. People change their minds or lose their courage.

Interviewing detectives

Active. Whether an active detective will talk to you depends on the detective and department policy. Some will (perhaps if you agree to confidentiality), many won't. Some will speak to family, some won't. Interestingly, some will speak more freely to TV reporters.

Retired. Ex-detectives are a bonanza. They often have copies of file documents – *Look what one gave us!* – and they know things that aren't in the file. In one case, a retired detective revealed that a key piece of evidence (the fatal bullet) had been lost. In another, we were told that a victim's clothes had blown off a clothesline while police were drying them and were dragged off by a dog.

Interviewing experts

In many cold cases, non-police experts were consulted. It might have been crime lab personnel. Probation officer. Handwriting examiner. Fire inspector. Crime scene photographer. A surprising number keep their notes for years (especially in interesting cases).

If you need an expert to interpret information, they are out there – and free. Doctors, dentists, anthropologists, pathologists, metallurgists, firearms experts, psychologists, lawyers – you can find them through universities, Facebook groups, LinkedIn, Reddit, etc. We've had good luck getting free consultations on cold cases. It's usually a one-shot deal, it's interesting, and they want to help or be on a podcast.

Don't assume you (or police) know what a test result means. In one New Mexico case we worked, the victim's autopsy showed a high Blood Alcohol Concentration. Police assumed she drank a large amount of alcohol before her death. But we learned from an expert that the BAC was likely affected by decomposition (she was found after several days inside a hot car). Similarly, if you see only the victim's blood type in pre-DNA reports, keep in mind that the suspect might have been a non-secretor or had the same blood type.

Interviewing attorneys

Suppose your victim was involved in a criminal, divorce, or personal injury case. Most lawyers don't keep files for decades, but some do. We've spoken to more than one attorney who kept files with the dream of writing a book.

If you happen to know a lawyer, it might be better to ask him or her to make the outreach. Either way, lawyers know what they're allowed to do. We've had some give us case files with the understanding that a privilege review would be performed by one of our attorney volunteers.

Others might not have files but might remember your subject. In one case, a woman was last seen on a Monday. Court records showed she had been sued for a car accident, and her deposition (*sworn testimony*) had been taken the Friday before. The injured man's attorney remembered the victim well – not just because she vanished, but also because his client had told her he forgave her, and they had shared an uplifting moment.

Another attorney remembered this informative tale about a missing person: The attorney represented several men who lost their belongings in a fire. When the case settled, the attorney set up bank accounts for each claimant so they wouldn't have to carry cash around their sketchy apartment building. One declined, insisting on taking his nearly $3,000 in cash. Days later, police informed the attorney that his client – and the money – had vanished under circumstances suggesting foul play. He was never seen again.

Interviewing locals

Especially in smaller communities, talk to residents. We sometimes start with local librarians. They're good at identifying longtime residents who might be knowledgeable or interested. (Some have even made introductory calls for us.)

Locals hear rumors. They know the players. We visited one community where a schoolteacher was murdered more than 50 years earlier. The crime was still well known, in part because she had taught current residents' parents and grandparents. One longtime resident had been shown the suspect's tracks, which she remembered decades later because they were the biggest feet she ever saw.

Interviewing reporters

Retired reporters sometimes have information. Some still have their notebooks or photos they took, or they simply remember things they saw or heard at crime scenes. Their names are easy to find from your newspaper searches, and you can then try to locate them using Truthfinder, LinkedIn, Facebook, or regular internet searches.

Interviewing prisoners

Most prisoners can have visitors and make phone calls. NOTE: When speaking with a prisoner on the phone, remember the call is likely being recorded.

Federal prisons all follow the same process for visits. You can search the Bureau of Prisons inmate locator, https://www.bop.gov/inmateloc/, click on the name, and a link will open to request a visit.

With state prisons and local jails, there's no uniformity. All have visiting times (such as 9-11 a.m. or 1-3 p.m.). Some require appointments. Some will let you show up and ask for a visit; others require that the prisoner add you in advance to an approved visitor list. That might require you to write the prisoner and ask for a visit. If you know family, consider asking them to recommend a meeting. If you want to take an electronic device (such as a recorder or camera), you'll have to get permission from the administration.

Attorneys have a little more flexibility in visiting prisoners. Some prisons prohibit an attorney visit unless the prisoner's criminal attorney authorizes it. In our view, that is improper. Prisoners have a right to speak with attorneys. Indeed, many prisoners no longer have an assigned criminal attorney, especially if they've been incarcerated for 10+ years.

Keep in mind that prisoners can have valid information but can also be unreliable. Prisoners have been known to fabricate information (such as a suspect's confession) to seek earlier release or catch a break on other charges. All information should be corroborated. NOTE: Law enforcement cannot use jailhouse informants as their agents. Informants must act on their own or with a private party. So if *you* (a private person) arrange for an informant to pump his cellie for information, the information can be used. But don't be surprised if the prisoner asks you to describe his helpfulness at an upcoming parole hearing.

Interviewing suspects

The above considerations apply if you are interviewing a potential person of interest. Interviewing suspects is important not just to obtain information, but also to apply pressure. (By "interviewing", we're including conversations in other contexts, such as pretexts where the subject believes you are asking for help in identifying people from a class photo, or just reaching out to everyone who lived in the neighborhood.)

When interviewing a potential suspect, you should take precautions. Avoid meeting in a private location. Be very familiar with the case file so that any discrepancies are noted immediately. It's especially important not to interrupt suspects when they are talking about the crime.

Some suspects ("helpful criminals") want to involve themselves in the investigation, perhaps due to a controlling nature or to deflect attention from themselves. They want to direct conversations, suggest theories, or next steps. They might even request the investigation and might become impatient if your investigation doesn't seem to be moving in the direction they want. You should avoid disclosing details about the case, especially "holdbacks" (*information withheld from the general public*).

Depending on the circumstances, you can feed suspects misinformation, perhaps to lull them into believing that you do not suspect them or to induce them to take action. A classic example is the 1970 murder of Loretta Jones in Carbon County, Utah. Decades later, Det. David Brewer announced that Loretta's body had been exhumed and DNA was being obtained. The announcement alone caused the suspect to panic and reveal himself. We occasionally ask persons of interest if they will provide DNA. We've also announced searches for a body and then surveilled suspects to see if they went to a suspicious location.

Visiting crime scenes

Try to visit the crime scene or have someone walk it while you observe. Even if a structure no longer exists, a visit will convey a sense of distance, angles, and other information that is hard to envision from words alone.

At this scene, it was all too easy to figure out how the killer climbed through a window into this victim's home:

In this next image, the heavy metal lid and deep below-ground

chamber behind a department store caused us to doubt the official theory that our tiny victim removed the lid, climbed down into the  water-filled cavity to get warm, then balanced on a narrow bar to replace the lid over her head. (We were even more skeptical because the victim's apartment was only a few hundred yards away; we could see it from where we were standing.) We discuss this case in our *Cold Case Talk* episode "Cami Shepherd: Undetermined".

In another case, we wondered how a suspect could have removed a victim from a busy motel complex without anyone noticing. Then we went there. Immediately adjacent to the victim's motel room was a convenient – and discreet – parking area. Back up the  suspect's van, carry the victim out the back door, and no one would see. (The fence was added years later, according to the helpful motel owner.)

SECTION VII

PUBLICIZING THE CASE

This section discusses publicity that is intended to help solve a case. Although we have our own podcast (*Cold Case Talk*), we don't pretend to be podcasting experts. But publicity can be very helpful with cold cases.

During our first meeting with Salt Lake City police about Rosie Tapia's 1995 murder, a lieutenant told us, "If it were up to me, we'd have a 24-hour Rosie Channel." Tips come in every time a story runs on Rosie's case, he explained.

Publicity can generate leads, correct misinformation, and keep cases in the public mind.

Local media

How can you get local media interested in your case? Here are some ideas that have worked for us. NOTE: Assume you are being recorded or that a reporter might use anything you say, unless you have an express agreement to be "off the record" or "background only".

Does a local station have a regular "justice files" feature? Contact them. You're making their job easier if you bring an interesting case to their attention and can provide a family member or investigator to appear on camera.

Most local newspapers are interested in crime stories, especially if they don't have to go looking for them. Their websites have contact information for reporters or the news desk. NOTE: TV folks read newspapers. If they see an article about your case, they might pitch it to their editors.

Do you have a local Crime Stoppers that does a regular "Crime of the Week" feature? Ask them to add your case.

Consider local radio news. In addition to their own listeners, they're often associated with a TV station so they might also give their TV colleagues a heads up.

National media

In our experience, getting the attention of national media often requires a pre-existing relationship or new information on a high-profile case. The growing number of true crime shows offers opportunities to submit summaries of your interesting case, mentioning the availability of family members, detectives, and other witnesses. Local media coverage can transition into national coverage, particularly if the story is picked up by outlets like the Associated Press.

Podcasts

Many podcasts focus on cold cases. Virtually all states and large cities have local podcasters who can generate interest (including by law enforcement), elicit information, and keep the event in the public mind. National podcasts serve the same function if you can interest them in your case. One of our favorites is *The Deck*, which explores diverse and less-publicized cases. It has covered three of our cases, one of which produced a tip for us hours after the episode aired.

Social media

Social media is an excellent means to find evidence or witnesses. New leads are generated by new exposure and repeated exposure to the public. Also, someone with information about a case often starts by searching to see if it has already been solved.

Facebook has a more "mature" demographic, which can be helpful with older cold cases. Younger people might have a Facebook profile, but might post more often on places like Instagram, TikTok, YouTube, etc. These social media sites pull up well in search engines and provide an easy way to communicate privately (messaging).

Effective crowdsourcing must convey legitimacy. The audience needs to believe that contacting you is safe. In one case, a subject's estranged wife got our message and Googled us, so she knew we were legit. But she wanted to be sure it was really us and not an imposter. We directed her to one of our personal Facebook pages, where we posted a coded message. She saw it, and we went from there.

One effective method is creating a separate page for a specific death or disappearance. These might be titled "Where is Betty Hudson?" or "Who Killed Leslie O'Brien?" (We sometimes elect not to use "Justice for…" because it's used in many circumstances other than unsolved cases. However, the word "justice" does have emotional appeal.)

With a high number of references to the subject, the page shows up higher on search results. It's frequently shared or attracts media attention, especially in smaller communities.

Facebook posts can be "boosted": You pay to have your post aimed at specific locations, people of specific genders or age groups, or who list specific interests. We get very high engagements in smaller or more rural communities.

Pictures grab attention. Try to include 2+ images, especially if one shows the victim in unusual attire such as a graduation gown or uniform. Be sensitive; it is offensive in some cultures (for example, some Native American tribes) to post photographs without family consent.

We recommend against emphasizing a specific theory in your post unless you're pretty confident or want to apply pressure.

Monitor comments. In one of our cases, a man had been convicted of a "no body" murder but still proclaimed his innocence. We wanted to find the body. The man's family got into a vicious fight with his ex-girlfriend on our Facebook page. A family member finally let slip that "It wouldn't have happened if you'd kept your legs shut, [*expletive deleted*]." (Those same folks threatened to sue us if we didn't take down our post. We declined.)

Also watch comments in case someone messes up your strategy. In one case, a witness gave us information about a suspect's car. We decided to do a public post asking for the same information, hoping to get confirmation or generate a previously unknown source. The original witness left an annoyed comment, "I already told you the car was red!" We don't usually hide comments, but we hid that one. We then privately explained to her that we made the post to try to flush out more witnesses.

Take screen shots or download anything interesting. While looking for a missing vehicle associated with a case, a commenter replied to our post with, "Didn't the FBI already pick up that car?" We contacted him immediately, and among other things learned a description of the driver. Shortly afterward, the witness deleted his question.

Consider posting on other high-interest pages (or asking others to do so if it's members-only). For example:

High school class/reunion pages. The murder or disappearance of a classmate can remain a topic of interest for years. Classmates might have insight but were never interviewed. Interestingly, police sometimes share extra information when it is to update classmates at a reunion.

Local town/city pages. There are thousands of local-interest Facebook pages. Read enough to be sure a post would be appropriate. Members might have photos of buildings, streets, etc. around the time of your case.

Cold case pages. Many locations have Facebook pages dedicated to cold cases. A few examples include https://www.facebook.com/EastIdahoColdCases (Idaho), https://www.facebook.com/iowacoldcases (Iowa), and https://www.facebook.com/profile.php?id=100089103616888 (Utah). These pages can generate interest and exposure. Ask the page administrator to post something about your case or offer to write something.

Interest/hobby pages. Experts in waiting! In one case, police could not identify an unusual watch found at a crime scene. Decades later, we posted a picture on a Timex collectors' page and had the answer within 24 hours.

Fundraising pages. Look for GoFundMe or other crowdfunding pages related to your person's death or disappearance.

SECTION VIII

COLD CASE DNA: MYTHS AND REALITIES

This section is not a primer on forensic DNA; that would fill volumes. Instead, we'll try to clear up misconceptions and answer common questions specific to cold cases. For more information or to send us questions about DNA, check out our website www.ColdCaseDNA.com.

Our qualifications for discussing cold case DNA include our own experiences when investigating cases, our ongoing review of DNA-related court cases in the United States, and our founding of a state-of-the-art forensic DNA laboratory in Salt Lake City, Intermountain Forensics (IMF). *See* www.IntermountainForensics.com. NOTE: We do not speak for IMF, which is now a separate nonprofit and might or might not agree with views stated in this book.

Does everyone who is arrested give a DNA sample?

Sort of. All states require persons arrested on suspicion of certain offenses to provide a DNA sample upon arrest. It's usually limited to persons arrested for felonies or Class A (the most serious) misdemeanors.

In most states, an arrestee's DNA must be deleted if charges are not brought or are dropped, or the person is acquitted. Most states make this difficult, however, so it doesn't usually happen. In one case, a court ordered a Florida man's DNA to be removed from the system. It wasn't, and years later it produced a hit in another case. A second court ruled that the DNA could be used despite the fact that keeping it in the system was a violation of the first court's order.

Is there a database with the DNA of everyone who has been arrested?

Sort of. There's a nationwide DNA database called CODIS. CODIS is short for Combined DNA Index System. It contains DNA profiles generated by what we'll shorthand as "STR" testing. This is traditional DNA testing that has been used for decades. As of April 2021, CODIS had 14,541,796 profiles of persons convicted of a crime, 4,341,864 profiles of arrested persons, and 1,103,683 forensic (crime scene or missing person) profiles.

CODIS was not developed until the late 1990s, and it wasn't until the mid-2010s that most states authorized the collection of DNA from pre-conviction arrestees. (Some states didn't do it even after the law allowed it.) So CODIS has limitations in helping with older cold cases.

Would more cold cases be solved if DNA from prisoners were added to CODIS?

Sure. But getting DNA from a prisoner requires a warrant. That is because – unlike someone who leaves DNA at a crime scene or tosses a cigarette in the trash – prisoners do not voluntarily "abandon" their DNA just by being in prison. To get a prisoner's DNA, law enforcement must show probable cause to believe he committed a crime different from the one for which he is incarcerated, and that his DNA would help resolve it. (One exception might apply: Some courts have ruled that, if giving a DNA sample was part of the prisoner's sentence but it wasn't collected for some reason, law enforcement can collect it now. You might mention that if you are presenting a lead to officials that involves a presently incarcerated suspect.)

Is there a new type of DNA testing that can identify unknown suspects?

Yes. For purposes of our discussion, we'll shorthand the newer DNA testing as "SNP" testing. This is sometimes called "Golden State Killer" or "genetic genealogy" testing. SNP testing includes whole genome sequencing, Kintelligence, microarrays, and other types of sequencing. These methods can produce DNA profiles that can be uploaded to the sites GEDmatch, www.GEDmatch.com, and FamilyTreeDNA, www.FamilyTreeDNA.com. In March 2023, a new nonprofit database called the DNA Justice Foundation, https://www.dnajustice.org/, was launched by pioneers CeCe Moore *(Parabon NanoLabs)*, Margaret Press *(DNA Doe Project)* and Kevin Lord *(Intermountain Forensics)*.

What do the genealogists do next?

Once the SNP profiles are uploaded, the GEDmatch, FamilyTreeDNA, and DNA Justice sites identify DNA relatives, people who have consented to their DNA being compared by law enforcement. The genealogists then do what genealogists do: They look at census records, newspaper stories, city directories, death records, etc., to find out how the relative is related to the person with the unidentified DNA.

One of the first cases solved with the help of genetic genealogy was the Canal Killer in Phoenix. That case was resolved in 2015 through a lead provided by Dr. Colleen Fitzpatrick of Identifinders using the killer's Y chromosome. In 2018, the infamous Golden State Killer case was closed with the arrest of Joseph DeAngelo. Genealogists had found relatives that (based on the amount of shared DNA) were probably third cousins to the killer. They researched the

Not so...

Some people think DNA profiles created for cold cases are uploaded to sites like Ancestry.com, MyHeritage.com or 23andMe. Nope! Customers choose to have their DNA tested on those sites. They then choose to upload their profiles to GEDmatch, FamilyTreeDNA, or DNAJustice.

relatives' family trees until they identified a potential suspect. Law enforcement took it from there.[6]

Under current guidelines, no one is supposed to be arrested based solely on the work of genetic genealogists. Their work produces a lead, a "tip". Basically, "Have you looked at this person?" Law enforcement takes it from there, independently confirming or ruling out the subject. They might ask him for a DNA sample or (in the U.S.) follow him and pick up an abandoned napkin or cigarette. That sample can then be subjected to traditional STR testing by an accredited lab for official comparison.

Is searching these public databases constitutional?

Probably. While there is academic and online debate, every court so far has ruled that the suspect "abandoned" his DNA at the crime scene, and it is being compared to the DNA of people who have "consented" to it.

---

[6] For an interesting account of this groundbreaking work, see *I Know Who You Are: How an Amateur DNA Sleuth Unmasked the Golden State Killer and Changed Crime Fighting Forever* by Barbara Rae-Venter (2023).

*Coalition cofounder Jason Jensen obtains a voluntary DNA sample
from the relative of a deceased person of interest*

Is SNP testing (genetic genealogy) used in all cases?

Not presently. It's not needed in most cases. Step 1 is
traditional STR testing. If that produces a hit, either to CODIS
or to a known person, no further testing is needed.

SNP testing is more expensive than traditional STR testing. It
might also have limitations if the sample is a "mixture"
(contains biological information from more than one person). It
depends on the case, quality of the sample, whether a
comparison sample is available, etc. SNP testing is very
effective with single-source samples such as bones, teeth,
semen, or blood. For example, differential extraction
(*separating sperm cells from skin cells*) can often produce
single-source sperm cell profiles. SNP testing can also be

useful when a mixture is of two people of different genders (for example, semen mixed with a female victim's DNA).

What is an MVac and does it work?

An MVac System is a DNA collection machine. It's basically a small DNA-sucking vacuum. The MVac has been used successfully on shell casings, rocks, jewelry, hats, and a wide range of other surfaces. One FBI study suggested that MVacs can extract up to 12x more DNA than traditional swabbing. Depending upon the conditions, individual swabs might first be attempted.

What factors affect usability of cold case DNA?

A number of factors can affect the adequacy of a DNA sample. Some of the most common include:

- Age. Samples can degrade over time.
- Storage. Temperature (especially heat), humidity, light, and other conditions can affect viability.
- Contamination. Improper handling or exposure to bacteria or fungi can contaminate a sample.
- Type. Different sample types (for example, blood and saliva) have different levels of DNA quality and quantity. Rootless hair is tricky but can be done.
- Time. The time between collection and extraction can affect the quality and amount of DNA obtained.
- Inhibitors. Proteins, salts, detergents and other inhibitors can affect the quality and quantity of DNA obtained.

What is accreditation and why does it matter?

"Accreditation" is the independent third-party evaluation of a laboratory's management system against a set of recognized standards which ensures that the laboratory is competent and equipped to perform forensic testing. This means subjecting the lab to a thorough and regular assessment of its methods, equipment, staff, and protocols. The lab's system of maintaining confidentiality, impartiality, and efforts toward constant improvement, referred to as a management system, are also assessed. (DNA is a valuable commodity, and confidentiality accreditation standards create a structure that should prevent DNA profiles or data being sold or licensed to third parties.) The typical set of standards applied to forensic testing laboratories are the ISO/IEC 17025 standards for testing and calibration laboratories, often with additional forensic specific standards that address specific considerations for forensic science.

Courts expect laboratories that perform forensic STR testing to have ISO/IEC 17025 accreditation. Some agencies do not (yet) require accreditation for SNP testing and only a handful of lab systems have ISO/IEC 17025 accreditation in this type of SNP testing, such as Intermountain Forensics, DNA Labs International, University of Nebraska Medical Center, and the

Center for Human Identification at the University of North Texas. Due to the small number of laboratories with ISO/IEC 17025 accreditation, some organizations use labs that hold other forms of accreditation such as Clinical Laboratory Improvement Act (CLIA) or Association for the Advancement of Blood and Biotherapies (AABB).

As more cases are resolved using leads produced by Forensic Investigative Genetic Genealogy and SNP testing, criminal defendants are increasingly challenging the entire process, and we believe courts will expect ISO/IEC 17025 accreditation for SNP testing sooner than later.

Why is forensic DNA testing so expensive?

One huge barrier to solving cold cases is that SNP testing is too expensive. It takes years to start a DNA laboratory, especially if it goes through the process of accreditation. The equipment and chemicals used for testing are expensive. And, if a lab is for-profit, there must be a return on investment.

The public can donate toward DNA testing costs. Donations to 501(c)(3) nonprofits, such as Intermountain Forensics, DNA Doe Project, National Center for Missing and Exploited Children (NCMEC), Seasons of Justice, Vegas Justice League, etc., are tax deductible.

But donations and existing funding can only go so far. The cost of DNA testing must come down. This might require more nonprofits, more government grants, and perhaps the use of combined purchasing power to lower costs.

SECTION IX
MISSING PERSONS

In keeping with our cold case focus, this book doesn't dive too deeply into "hot" missing persons cases. But these can turn cold, and there are some things that should be done right away.

This discussion is limited to missing persons over the age of 18. Unlike adults, children do not have a "right to go missing" and police will investigate. (Fortunately, nearly 99% of children who go missing are found within 48 hours.)

How to get law enforcement
to investigate your missing adult

This is not a detailed primer on how to work current missing persons cases. You need law enforcement to work the case. They have far greater resources. They can monitor credit card use in real time. They can have a cellular service provider "ping" her phone. They can check carpool lane sensors and vehicle GPS data.

Law enforcement sometimes decline to investigate missing adults or will only do so for a short period. That's because adults have a "right to disappear" – it's not a crime to leave without telling anyone. However, law enforcement *will* investigate if they believe foul play is involved or the person is in imminent danger. You should "make a case" to them early and often. Things you can point out include:

- The obvious: blood, signs of a struggle, etc.

- Behavior changes: Your son calls daily but hasn't since Sunday. His friends haven't heard from him. He didn't show up for work. He hasn't posted on social media.

- Other red flags: Her pet was alone without extra food or water. She wasn't home when her children got home. Her apartment was unlocked. Her purse (medication, eyeglasses, etc.) aren't with her. Etc.

Give police the contact information for friends or an employer who can confirm that this is not normal. Show them the daily Instagram posts that suddenly stopped.

Be up front if you suspect your missing adult was involved with illegal or risky activities. That might make police more likely to suspect that foul play has occurred.

Media and social media

If law enforcement won't open a case, try the news media. They often will cover a missing person regardless of how police classify it. It adds pressure to investigate. It spreads the word. It generates tips. If your loved one is voluntarily gone, media coverage might persuade him to let you know he's all right.

Offer multiple pictures in different settings. Be prepared to go down a lot of rabbit holes. Missing person reports generate a lot of "sightings," most of which turn out to be dead ends. But at least it's a lead. Social media typically do not produce as wide a reach, but they are sometimes more likely to reach acquaintances.

Searches

Searches are critical immediately after a disappearance. Notify the media and post on social media that you will be conducting a search. Mention that volunteers are needed, when to meet, where to meet, and emphasize that even short periods of time can help. Have maps or grids ready to assign so that people won't duplicate efforts.

Knock on doors near the missing person's residence, common hang out spots, or last known location. Have two or more photos ready to show, if possible. Ask about video surveillance cameras (like Ring doorbells) – remember they might be set to erase on a regular basis.

Some communities have nonprofit groups experienced with searches. This might include search dogs, drones, "grid" searches, and other efforts. Local grocery stores might donate food or water for searches. If you can't find an organization through a Google search, call a local law enforcement agency. They often know groups that will help set up searches.

Coalition volunteers lower a camera into a mine shaft while searching for Susan Powell in Utah's west desert.

Consider a private investigator and OSINT investigator

Private investigators can be very helpful in missing person cases. They'll jump on it. Their efforts don't usually interfere with law enforcement. They have resources not available to most private citizens. For example, they often have high-level tracking services like TLOxp, license plate readers, and arrest monitors. They're good at finding video and witnesses. People will talk to them. OSINT investigators can do amazing things with online and electronic records. National programs such as *We Help the Missing* track PIs who will work for reduced or no cost.

If you have access to the missing person's phone / computer / iPad, look at every app to review message capability. For example, Gmail now offers a Chat feature. Other examples include texting, email, WhatsApp, Kik, Viber, Instagram, Snapchat, GroupMe, Slack, Discord, and most gaming apps.

If loved ones can't figure out how to get into the missing person's computer, an investigator can probably help. NOTE: Many people use work-related computers. Employers usually have passwords and might be willing to give you access or search it themselves.

Fraud alerts

If you're named on an account, consider submitting a fraud alert to the missing person's bank or credit card issuers. This will draw attention if someone else tries to use the card, and perhaps convince a voluntarily absent person to call if he suddenly can't use his own card. Alerts are instant: One of our Board members called her bank when her car and wallet were stolen. The thief drove there to try to pass a check, and bank officials stalled until the police arrived. (Unfortunately, the woman's accomplices later murdered her to keep her quiet. They were convicted of the murder and a felony car theft ring.)

Emergency court proceedings to get information

Even if they want to help, police often can't get a warrant because it's not illegal for adults to disappear in the United States. Without probable cause to believe a crime has been committed, their hands are tied.

Loved ones must act *immediately* or evidence will be lost forever. One key example: cell phone triangulation records (showing approximate locations). These are destroyed in 60-90 days. Carriers will provide this data with a court order (or without one if you are on the account).

So how do you get a court order? An emergency lawsuit might be required. In one case, we filed a quick probate action. In another, we had the missing person's mother file suit against the missing person. To get an emergency order, we had to make the legal argument that the missing person was in possession of his mother's iPad which was in danger of being destroyed.[7]

A premature lawsuit for declaration of death (*discussed more below*) might also work – whatever it takes to get an emergency motion in front of a judge. You must act immediately; it takes time to prepare these.

When her 27-year-old son Justin went missing in 2017, Marilyn had no idea that his cell phone data would be erased so quickly. Marilyn later joined the Coalition board to help educate others.

---

[7] You can explain what's really going on in your court filing. In our case where a mother "sued" her missing son, we made clear that she loved her son, did not really care about the iPad, and just needed a way to get into court to request an order for cell phone data before it was destroyed. Check with an attorney.

NamUs, Find a Grave, BillionGraves

An invaluable resource in older missing persons cases is NamUs.gov. It contains thousands of entries for missing persons and unidentified bodies. Any registered user can enter a missing person case into NamUs, which is helpful if police will not open a case. However, NamUs will not post the case unless law enforcement verifies it and authorizes it to be published.

NamUs also has an "unidentified persons" category. Search options include location last seen, date of last contact, descriptions, tattoos, etc.[8] NOTE: Race and ethnicity might be guesses on NamUs. Gender might even be wrong if remains are incomplete. In 2023, Intermountain Forensics extracted DNA and performed SNP testing on skeletal remains long believed to be those of a woman. He actually turned out to be a man who had disappeared decades earlier.

Check with local coroners and medical examiners; they'll have information on unidentified bodies in their jurisdictions that haven't been entered into NamUs.

Cemetery databases like Find a Grave and BillionGraves include John and Jane Does and are updated regularly. NOTE: If you suspect the identity of an unidentified body, consider checking Ancestry.com and other genealogy websites that have family trees. Genealogists occasionally mention when family members are missing or list an "approx." death date.

---

[8] You can start more narrowly, but if you don't find what you're looking for, expand your search. Remember that ethnicity, hair color, height, etc., might be hard to determine in some cases.

Declarations of death / estate administration

All states have a process by which someone can be declared dead. If a body has not been found, a declaration of death might be the only way to get benefits under a life insurance policy or recover other assets. A declaration of death can also help a cold case investigation in other ways.

Once someone is declared dead, a court can appoint a representative of that person's estate. The representative has access to bank records, cell phone records, credit card records, GPS locators in a subject's car, Smart TV and Alexa-type device data, medical records, social media accounts, employment records, life insurance records, DNA testing the subject might have submitted, and other records if they still exist.

Declarations of death basically require a court petition explaining where/when the alleged decedent was last seen, how long it has been since the last contact, important family events he would normally have attended if he were alive, etc. All heirs must be notified.

If there's been no known contact for a certain period of time (usually 5-10 years depending on the state's law), the subject is assumed to be dead. You can try to get a declaration of death earlier, but you'll have a higher burden of proof because there won't be a presumption of death. That doesn't mean you can't try; it just means that the judge might require some pretty convincing evidence to be persuaded that the person is actually deceased.

No-body homicide prosecutions

The lack of a confirmed death does not necessarily prevent prosecution. Per the site http://www.nobodycases.com, as of January 2023, 576 homicide cases have gone to trial in the U.S. without a body. Obviously there are hurdles. Time and place of death are usually unknown, and cause of death is more difficult to prove. Nonetheless, the conviction rate is high, usually aided by some combination of physical evidence (blood, shell casings, etc.), witnesses, confessions, suspicious activities, and motive.

SECTION X
YOU'VE BUILT YOUR CASE – NOW WHAT?

Y ou've gathered information from online sources, court records, interviews, etc. Now you're wondering what you can do with it.

Can your evidence be used in court?

Probably. A few issues might arise, including:

Searches. As a private citizen, your actions are not governed by the Constitution. The Fourth Amendment only regulates governmental action. If you snoop in someone's garage without a warrant, evidence you find won't be excluded on the grounds that it was a warrantless search (unless law enforcement asked you to do it).

Chain of custody. Don't worry too much about this. Chain of custody basically just means there's reason to believe that the matter (document, evidence, etc.) is what you say it is. It's a low standard. That's why it's fairly rare for evidence to be excluded on chain of custody grounds.

- Victim's mother hands you a doll. She says she found it on her child's grave 20 years ago. Mother's testimony would be enough to support a finding that it was a doll found on Victim's grave.

- Suspect hands you a cigarette butt. He says he found it on the ground outside Victim's window but forgot to give it to the police. His story would support a finding that it is a cigarette butt found outside Victim's window. That's enough for a chain-of-custody threshold. (Whether a jury believes the story is another question.)

What if you've built a case but no one will listen?

You've outlined your evidence and sources. You show law enforcement your rock solid case – but they won't act. What are your options?

First, keep in mind that law enforcement might not be ignoring you. Just as you might keep your investigation private, law enforcement will not necessarily tell you if they are following up on your lead.

Also keep in mind that law enforcement might not *disagree* with you, but they must have sufficient *proof.* Unsuccessful searches divert resources. (How many backhoes have been rented to look for Jimmy Hoffa since 1975?) Unsuccessful trials are costly and might bar future prosecutions under principles of double jeopardy.

Higher-level review. Some states have a process to go over an agency's head and get an "independent" review of the case. Typically, this can be requested only by a victim or immediate family member. In some states, this might include a chance to argue your case directly to the reviewer. In others, all you can request is for them to look at the original file material plus your new information.

Third party review. Consider showing your proof to a third party already known to law enforcement, perhaps a cold case organization or crime reporter. They might have connections.

Wrongful death lawsuit. Heirs can try to get answers (or justice) through wrongful death lawsuits. Think O.J. Simpson – he was acquitted of murder charges, but later lost a wrongful death suit brought by the victims' families. There are hurdles. What is the statute of limitations, and was it extended because no one was ever charged? Can you prove the cause of death? Will confidential sources go public? Will a lawyer take the case? A lawsuit lets you use the court system to get information. You can subpoena the subject's credit card records, GPS data, Google searches, cell phone records, if they still exist. You can question him under oath. If he "takes the Fifth" and refuses to testify, you can use that against him in a civil lawsuit.

Objection to inheritance. If a perpetrator seeks to be (or has been) appointed administrator of an estate or is a named beneficiary, an objection can be filed that she is not eligible because she caused the victim's death. NOTE: An objection must usually be filed by someone with a personal interest (such as immediate family, or someone who would receive a bigger share of the estate or become the beneficiary of a life insurance policy). Whether a conviction is required to disqualify the perpetrator depends on the state.

Citizen's Grand Jury. Most states have something called a citizen's grand jury. If the government won't prosecute, you can take your case to a specially appointed group of citizens or judges. The procedure varies by state. In 2021, a Kansas woman was allowed to present allegations of rape to a citizen's grand jury by gathering hundreds of signatures. In Utah, you sign up on a website to present your case to five judges who meet quarterly. These citizens' grand jury laws have been around for centuries, but they're still on the books and you can use them.

Post-death declaration of probable cause. If the evidence is strong enough, a prosecutor might provide the family with a posthumous (*post-death*) statement of probable cause. The prosecutor states that, based upon the evidence, she believes the perpetrator has been identified and would have brought charges. It gives the victim's family some degree of closure.

Exhumation. It's tough, but private citizens can obtain exhumations. (One of our founders exhumed her grandfather, a 1963 cold case.) The requirements are too complex and state-specific for this book, but generally it requires a permit, consent of heirs, and a cooperative funeral home, DNA lab director, coroner or medical examiner, or combination thereof.

Publicity. As discussed earlier, news media and social media are very valuable when investigating cold cases. The same is true after you've built your case. Reporters won't just accept your conclusions, of course. They'll want proof of who, what, when, where, why, and how. You can also make a case directly on social media, which might get picked up by local news. If you're going to name a living suspect, be careful to explain your reasoning to avoid a lawsuit – see our discussion below in Risks of Working Cold Cases.

SECTION XI

INNOCENCE CHALLENGES

Every case where a defendant is wrongfully incarcerated is a cold case. If you believe someone was wrongfully convicted, you have a few options. Most of these require cooperation from the prisoner or his lawyer.

Approximately 100 counties and states have created "conviction integrity/review units". As of mid-2022, more than half of these have not (yet) produced an exoneration. But a prisoner can at least try them.

Other options are "innocence" nonprofits, classes, or clinics. If a local college doesn't have an innocence program, suggest one. Your request might get further if you have support from someone the school would consider an authority on investigations or cold cases.

Innocence projects receive thousands of requests – far more than can be helped. Some programs are now limiting cases to those that can be solved by DNA. This is not just because they're easier, but also because prosecutors (and the public) are more persuaded by DNA exoneration than, for example, a witness changing her story. Also, a showing of actual innocence is usually required if the individual wants to seek compensation for his wrongful conviction.

If you're working on a suspected innocence case, you might assume that DNA testing will be made available if the government doesn't have to pay for it. Not necessarily. Every year, dozens of prisoners are exonerated by DNA. Nearly 200 of these were on death row, meaning that – but for the power of DNA – they might have been executed for crimes they did not commit. In many of these cases, prosecutors fought the new testing. Why? It wasn't money; defense lawyers or nonprofits typically offer to pay. Here are reasons that we have seen or heard:

- *DNA testing wouldn't be helpful.* Suppose a defendant admits physical interaction (such as sexual contact or striking another person). The only dispute might be whether there was consent or self-defense. DNA testing would not be informative here.

- *The request doesn't meet legal requirements.* All states allow post-conviction testing, and in 2023 the Supreme Court issued a ruling that will enable more requests. Prisoners must show that they would not have been convicted if favorable results had been available, and that DNA was not tested or more advanced testing is now available. Some states make it really hard. A prisoner might argue: "Semen was left at the scene. I was not there. Therefore, testing the semen would likely exonerate me." Despite the logic of this argument, some judges say the prisoner is just "speculating".

- *The absence of DNA wouldn't exonerate the defendant.* Some prosecutors argue that DNA results would not exonerate a defendant because they think the crime was committed by more than one person. Even if the DNA came back to another man, it wouldn't prove the defendant wasn't there.

- *It might result in a reversal – but not factual exoneration.* Some DNA testing might not fully exonerate the prisoner but would be enough to entitle him to a new trial. Meanwhile, witnesses have died. The victim doesn't want to be retraumatized. A prosecutor might fear that a guilty person will be released solely because a new trial would be difficult if not impossible.

- *It will end the death penalty.* In 2019, a family petitioned for DNA testing in a heinous rape-murder case. Their loved one had been convicted and executed for the crime. A ruling by the state's highest court after the execution suggested that the defendant had wrongly been denied DNA testing. Citing new evidence pointing to another suspect and offering to pay for the testing, the family sought to clear their loved one's name. Prosecutors fought new testing – hard – and won. This case was closely followed because it raised the possibility that DNA would prove that an innocent man had been executed. If that happens, it will dramatically alter the death penalty debate in the U.S.

SECTION XII

RISKS OF WORKING COLD CASES

It goes without saying that, unless you're careful, there might be physical danger – for example, if you meet with a suspect or work with an informant. But what other risks are there? Private citizens don't have the same protections as government officials. Can you be sued? Can a prosecutor use your evidence? Can there be disputes over a reward?

Can you investigate a case or do a show without family permission?

Yes. It's done all the time. Whether it's advisable depends on the circumstances. Remember that families have been burned before. Their frustration might grow if you are unable to solve the crime, if you don't work exclusively on their case, or you end up developing a different theory.

Can you "screw up" a prosecution?

Theoretically. But if you're working a case that hasn't been solved for decades, or on a closed case, it's pretty hard for someone to argue that you prevented it from being solved.

One area of concern could be tainting an ID by suggesting a particular suspect or theory. Another could be handling of evidence. Private citizens can arrange Bluestar Forensic or DNA testing, but it's best to notify law enforcement if you find physical evidence you believe is important.

Can you secretly record conversations?

It depends on the state's law. Although you should check with a lawyer when in doubt, it is a common saying that if you receive the phone call, your state's law applies. If you make the call, the recipient's state law applies. Most states and the federal government are "one-party+": Only one of the parties to a conversation has to consent (and that party can be you). Other states, such as Florida and Pennsylvania, are "all party": every participant must consent to the recording. NOTE: Some of these statutes say that an illegal recording cannot be used for any purpose. Whether that means your private recording can (or can't) be used in a prosecution would be decided by a judge.

Consent is not required if a conversation is taking place in a public location where there is no reasonable expectation of privacy. Feel free to sit at a nearby table and record whatever you can hear with normal human hearing.

Can rewards cause problems?

Rewards are time-tested methods of getting information.

Philadelphia, December 10, 1772.
TEN POUNDS Reward.
A BURGLARY.
WHEREAS a Number of evil difpofed Perfons, in the Night, between the 9th and 10th Inftant, burglarioufly and felonioufly, broke open the Gallery Door of the THEATRE, tore off, and carried away the Iron Spikes, which divide the Galleries from the upper Boxes ; and had they not been detected, and put to Flight by the Servants of the Theatre, who dwell in the Houfe, would, there is Reafon to imagine, have compleated their malicious Defigns. In order, therefore, that the Perpetrators may be brought to Juftice, the above Reward is offered, to whoever will difcover any of the Perfons concerned in the faid Burglary, to be paid on their Conviction.
DAVID DOUGLASS.

Disputes do arise. What if more than one person provides information? Rewards were split in the Beltway sniper case, the rescue of Elizabeth Smart, the capture of a serial killer in Chicago, and many other cases. You can put conditions on a reward. What if an informant didn't know about the reward until afterward? Courts usually deny recovery.

NOTE: Defendants might argue that witnesses are tainted by rewards. In fact, that argument was (unsuccessfully) made in one case where our efforts led to the defendant's arrest for the murder of a young child. Most cases include corroborating evidence, however, and it is up to a jury to assess all witnesses' credibility.

Can you get sued?

Sure. People make threats all the time. In one case we're working, a man who was simply asked if he knew anything about his neighbor's disappearance responded with a whole smorgasbord of threats: He had contacted the sheriff's office (he said). And his personal attorney. And would be having the county attorney issue a restraining order. "Do not mention my name and do not contact me again," he warned. We moved him up our persons-to-check-out list.

Defamation

Entire books are written about defamation law; we'll just skim a few concepts pertinent to cold cases. Defamation is "publishing" (speaking or writing) a falsehood that harms a living person's reputation. Note that claims cannot be brought by heirs; if you name a suspect who is dead, defamation laws do not apply.

Insurance. Most defamation lawsuits fail, but they can be costly and stressful. Check with an insurance agent; many homeowners' and renters' policies cover defamation. If not, adding it is cheap (usually less than $15). It might not cover statements made as part of a business, but buying business insurance that covers defamation is surprisingly affordable.

Fact vs. opinions. We have a right to state opinions, but we can't just claim everything is an opinion. Do the words have a common meaning? Can they be proven true or false? "Doug Harvey is creepy" is an opinion; "Doug Harvey is a crook" might not be. Also, we're not allowed to imply that we're relying on facts not known to the listener. That's why it's important to offer reasons for your opinion; people can then judge for themselves. Examples:

> TikToker A: *"We all know Melanie's husband killed her."* She might claim this is just her opinion, but she doesn't mention any facts upon which the opinion is based. She's implying facts not known to the listener.

> TikToker B: *"I think Melanie's husband killed her. His alibi is weak. He was having an affair. They lived in a community property state, so he would lose a lot of assets if they divorced."* Much better.

Public figure / public issue. You have a strong defense if the person you supposedly defamed is a "public figure," or the statement involved an important public issue. A person can become an "involuntary" public figure by (for example) being involved with a murder. In these cases, the person must show not only that you made a false statement, but that you acted intentionally or recklessly. It's not enough to show that you just made a mistake.

Privileged statements. You have a legal right to make some statements. For example, statements made in or to a court are privileged no matter how awful. There might be a "common interest" privilege if the recipient has a legitimate need for the information (arguably including statements made to police or to a victim's family). CAUTION: Even if a statement is privileged, you can't share it with more people than necessary.

The good news: If you're sued, you get to interrogate – for hours – the person accusing you. The bad news: It'll cost up to $1,000 in court reporter fees to do it.

Malicious prosecution

Suppose your evidence results in criminal charges, but they're later dismissed or the defendant is acquitted. In most cases, you're protected because a decision to bring charges is made by the prosecutor, who acts independently. That's how a court ruled when the TV show *Cold Justice* was sued. An acquitted man claimed that his prosecutor was pressured to bring charges because producers said the episode otherwise would not air. The court was not persuaded.

You lose some protection if the evidence you provide is subject to challenge. In 2019, a university settled disputed allegations that its innocence clinic coerced a confession from a man who was exonerated 15 years later. *See* William B. Crawford, *Justice Perverted: How The Innocence Project at Northwestern University's Medill School of Journalism Sent an Innocent Man to Prison* (2015).

Disclosure of sensitive materials

Public information can usually be disclosed. Some states bar disclosure of post-death photos without family authorization. Whether this prohibition violates the First Amendment has not been resolved, but courts have sided with families. In 2018, for example, Kurt Cobain's widow prevented the release of his death photographs to a podcaster who believed the singer had been murdered.

If you receive records, you generally have a right to publish them. This is true even if the person who gave them to you broke the law (Search *Pentagon Papers* or watch *The Post*).

Invasion of privacy

As always, check with a lawyer if you have concerns. Invasion of privacy lawsuits have been successful in cases where a defendant unlawfully conducted background checks, obtained and disclosed medical records, and used facial recognition software in violation of a state law.

An invasion of privacy by false light occurs when you publish statements that place an individual in a false light if (1) the false light would be highly offensive and (2) you knew of or recklessly disregarded the falsity of the implications. Unlike defamation, the angry person does not have to prove the statements were technically false; it's what the statements are *implying* that matters.

This might sound like an easier claim than defamation. But deaths, disappearances, and crime are all matters of public importance. And we have First Amendment rights. So a person suing for invasion of privacy will usually have to show that you acted with "actual malice" (knowledge or recklessness). That's a very high standard. If you've done your investigation as described above, you'll be fine.

Can you go to jail?

Technically, yes. It's unlikely, but here are some situations that could arise:

Trespass. As a private individual, you can conduct warrantless searches. You can dig up someone's yard. The evidence can still be used in a later proceeding, but you can also be criminally charged. *(We had consent for this search of an overgrown pond and eventually ended up draining the whole thing.)*

Stolen evidence / documents. We mentioned earlier that the First Amendment to the U.S. Constitution generally lets you publish material that you receive, even if it was obtained illegally in the first place. The person who stole it can still be charged, however. In the Pentagon Papers case, the *Washington Post* was allowed to publish Vietnam War documents stolen by Daniel Ellsberg. But Ellsberg was criminally charged for the original theft.

SECTION XIII

SHOULD YOU FORM A COLD CASE ORGANIZATION?

Yes!

It's hard but it's important. Records won't be shared. Witnesses won't cooperate. Families will be frustrated that you haven't solved a case that law enforcement haven't solved in 25 years. *You'll* be frustrated because you can't put time in on all of the cases and law enforcement won't tell you if they're following up on the lead you sent them months ago. And, of course, when you are volunteers, you have to work around your daily obligations and scrounge for funds to do simple things like paying for copies of a case file.

But one day you'll watch loved ones reminisce, hopeful of finally getting answers about the traumatic event that changed their lives forever. You'll get a call from a volunteer who just found a witness or a big clue. Someone will answer a phone or open a door and tell you things she has been keeping inside for 40 years.

You'll hear from a retired investigator who has been thinking about the case and just remembered something.... You'll get a call from a detective indicating that he agrees with your analysis and the department is reopening a closed case. You'll change the victim's photo on a cold case website from a mug shot to the smiling face sent to you by a family member.

You'll meet caring people and enjoy working with folks like Anne here (*reviewing reports at a police station*). As an

organization, you can study a larger number of cases. You can spot patterns. You can see the same person showing up in other cases, which law enforcement did not realize back then because of limited communication. You can brainstorm with others.

We recommend a formal structure such as a Limited Liability

Company or corporation for your own protection, and to make it easier to submit proposals and payments (to government agencies, for example). We're biased, but being a 501(c)(3) nonprofit can help assure families and the community as to your motives. It also allows tax-deductible donations and might make you eligible for grants.

Law enforcement in the United States are understaffed and underbudgeted. You can help them

...give unidentified persons back their name

...identify persons of interest in violent crimes

...exonerate the wrongfully accused

...determine "undetermined" deaths

...reopen erroneously closed cases

Feel free to reach out; we'll tell you about our experiences.

Cold Case Coalition
ColdCaseHelp.com
Info@ColdCaseHelp.com
Facebook: Cold Case Coalition
Twitter: @ColdCaseHelp

Made in the USA
Coppell, TX
13 October 2023